My Hands Hold My Story

Bethany Swafford

Published by Bethany Swafford, 2018.

This is a work of fiction. Similarities to real people, places, or events are entirely coincidental.

MY HANDS HOLD MY STORY

First edition. July 9, 2018.

Copyright © 2018 Bethany Swafford.

Written by Bethany Swafford.

For my parents who taught me to love books

Chapter One

1874 My world became one of silence when I was six years old.

Where others would hear the creak of the swaying wood or the pounding of the horses who were pulling the stagecoach, I heard nothing at all. Whenever the other passengers—five in this coach— attempted to have some conversation, their mouths would open wide, and they would lift their chins, to raise their voices above the din.

Perhaps to onlookers, it was strange to see a sixteen year old girl traveling alone, let alone one who was deaf. However, I had been given little choice in the matter.

Across from me, the heavyset man mopped the sweat from his brow and said, "...mistake to come...this way." His gaze then shifted to the man beside me and nodded as though he agreed with something said.

The response he gave was, "Business. What else?" He glanced at me as he spoke those words.

I didn't always know how to read the body language of everyone around me; there were so many nuances to a person's facial expression. In fact, I wasn't as good as some of my former schoolmates, and I knew I would never be an expert at it. Most of the time it was a matter of guesswork, and this time I guessed he was wondering where I was going and why I was on the journey alone.

Even if I could have explained how it had happened, I don't think I would have. It would have involved putting into words what I had been through and faced every day, much less what had forced me to go west. As I thought about Aunt Ruth's death, tears welled up in my eyes, and I brushed at them. The only other woman in the stagecoach, however, spotted me. She reached over from where she was seated in the middle on the opposite side of the coach and patted my knee in a way meant to be comforting.

I shifted my gaze to the window next to me and stared at the passing scenery. Though ten years had passed, my deafness remained a daily struggle. It set me apart from the majority of the world and made everyone treat me as different.

Though the event that took my hearing will always stick out in my mind, many of the details are forever fuzzy. Fever will do that to a person's memory, I suppose.

At the time, Father was fighting in the War Between the States, and he had been gone for two years. It hadn't been comfortable with him away. Simon, three years older than I, stocked the shelves of our family's store and did whatever odd jobs he could find to help out, while Mother did needlework to fill the gap Father's absence caused in our income.

The fever struck us without warning. I have a slight recollection of being ill, of hearing wheezing and coughing nearby whenever I managed to fight my way out of the blackness that seemed determined to consume me. Strange nightmares haunted my sleep. And then, when I woke up, everything was silent.

It took several moments for me to recognize that something was not as it should be. I'm not entirely sure what it was that made me realize I couldn't hear a thing—was it seeing the door swinging open but no corresponding squeak of the hinges?— but I do remember how I reacted. I had screamed. My throat had vibrated with the action, and I didn't hear a single note.

And it wasn't Mother who flew to my side to comfort me; it was my Aunt Ruth. Because, as I would learn later, my mother and baby James had died that morning.

As quickly as that, our family of five was cut down to three. With Father gone, Simon and I had to stay with Aunt Ruth and her husband. Grief-stricken and panicked over the sudden loss of one of my main senses, I unequivocally labeled the time as the worst period of my life, made even worse when my father did return, injured from a battle.

These memories never failed to bring tears to my eyes, especially given what happened next. I shook my head, pushing away the feeling of being unwanted that followed me wherever I went. How I wished for something to occupy my mind! Though I had a novel on my lap, it was difficult to read the words in the moving stage, and so there was little else to occupy my mind besides the event that had sent me west.

The stagecoach gave a sudden jolt, and the passenger next to me squished me against the side of the coach. If I had been in the middle, I had no doubt I would have had elbows in both of my sides. As it was, it seemed to take the man longer than necessary to give me back what little bit of room I was entitled to.

As far as inappropriate advances, it was somewhat light compared to some I had faced since my journey had begun. The first part of my travels, where there had been rails for the train, I had been accompanied by a chaperone, Mrs. Jimson. That imposing lady reached Buffalo, New York, decided she'd had enough of traveling, and returned to Springfield, Massachusetts.

With nowhere to go but onward, I had forced myself to continue alone. Each new train connection had left my funds a little lighter. I could only hope that I had enough to get me all the way to Montana.

The stage began to slow down. We had reached the next station, and we had barely stopped before one of the passengers opened the door. He made a gesture for me to disembark first, which I was more than happy to do.

It was a relief to stand upright and move around some. To my left, two men were already at work removing the harnesses from the horses.

We would only have a short time to relieve ourselves, eat a meal, and stretch our legs before the stagecoach would continue on its way, with or without us. Unsure where to go, I waited until someone else began to walk towards the station as they would have heard the directions the driver would have called out as soon as we stopped.

The woman went in a different direction, away from the main building. I assumed she was going to the outhouse, and as that was where I wished to go first, I followed her. Also, it was preferable to being alone with all the men.

Fortunately, there were two outhouses, so I didn't have to wait. When I stepped back out, I discovered the skinny passenger who had been beside me right there. The sly smile on his face sent a chill down my spine. I took a step to the side to go around him.

Before I could take a step forward, he grabbed my arm. "Hello again," he said. His face was uncomfortably close to mine, making his words all too easy to read on his lips. The smell of his putrid breath made me gag, and I tried to jerk away from him.

Around others, I was treated with deference and respect, even when they discovered I was deaf. It was how ladies were treated in the west. This man wasn't the first who had tried to have "fun" by confronting me away from other people, however. He would discover that just because I couldn't hear did not mean I was not able to defend myself.

This particular time, though, I didn't have to. The other woman stepped out of the outhouse and proceeded to smack the man with her reticule, yelling at him if her body language was anything to go by.

The man released me and was quick to hurry away. Grateful for her help, I turned to the woman. I brought my hand up to my lips and then moved it out, mouthing the words at the same time so she would be sure to understand me. *Thank you.*

"We women...stick together, especially...west. I....Ruby Walters," she said with a broad smile. She looped her arm around mine and pulled me towards the main building.

"I am Ivy Steele," I managed to say in response. It felt good to have someone on my side, at least for the moment.

AUNT RUTH'S HEAD WAS tilted at an unnatural angle, and her eyes stared at nothing.

With a start, I woke from the nightmare. Everyone else was still asleep, the swaying of the coach not bothering them, or they had grown accustomed to the movement. Breathing out, I leaned my head back, trying not to cry.

Would I ever be able to think of what had happened without losing my composure? Did I want to be so jaded to life and loss? Though only two months had passed since the accident, I didn't think it would ever happen.

Though I was tired, I was not able to get any more sleep that night in the moving stage. Every time I closed my eyes, I saw the same thing: Aunt Ruth lying at the bottom of the staircase. Instead of torturing myself, I stared out into the dark, knowing every mile brought me closer to my father.

It wouldn't be easy for me to become part of the family, this I knew very well. After all, three years previous, my father had sent a letter to inform me that he had remarried. So I had a stepmother to learn about while I became reacquainted with my older brother and father.

Leaving me in Springfield with Aunt Ruth must have made the most sense at the time, but ten long years had made for creating a significant divide in our family. Yes, I received a letter from Father every few months, but I felt no real connection to him. His life had taken a different course than mine.

Perhaps being in the same household would bring about a reconciliation between us. Or would my deafness make things worse than ever?

Uneasy thoughts about what the future would hold for me went round and round my head for most of the night.

It was mid-morning when the stage arrived in a small town. It was time for the last change to a different stagecoach line, and I parted company with the kind woman who was continuing on. She handed me a card and made sure I understood if I ever was in need, I could come to her and she would set me up in her business.

Given that being a lady of the night would ruin me forever, I wasn't keen on taking her up on the offer but thanked her just the same. In any event, I was only a week away from reaching the small town where Father and Simon lived. What need would I have for a job?

My carpet bag in one hand and my slate in the other, I hurried to the stage office. It took about five minutes, which was fast compared to some clerks I'd had to deal with in the past, but I managed to get the information I needed. The stage I had to take would not leave until noon the next day, meaning I needed a place to stay that night.

The clerk was kind enough to point me in the direction of the hotel and called over a young man to carry my trunk to the building. As ever, I tried to walk with confidence and kept a sharp watch on everyone I passed. Most men would tip their hat, and I would make sure to nod in return.

As I walked, the scents that could only be associated with a small town drifted on the breeze: horse manure, cooking food, the unmistakable smell of unwashed bodies as men passed by. Since I lost my hearing, my other senses often felt as though they were doubled, and so scents at times were overwhelming. I was relieved to reach the hotel.

A dollar got me a room for the night, and I was more than grateful to have some time to myself, although my dwindling funds concerned me. There was no time to send clothing to someone to launder, but I was able to spot-clean my traveling dress and let it air out.

Dressed in only my underclothes, I stretched out on the bed. With a sigh, I closed my eyes to take advantage of the time I had to sleep. The events of May were never far off from my mind even though I knew there was nothing I could do about them now. I could only hope that I had done all I could at the time, but I did wonder whether I would ever be satisfied.

THE LUMPS IN THE BED did not keep me from sleeping away the late afternoon, though I was achy when I woke up. The room had become stuffy as I had kept the window shut to keep out the dust.

I stretched as I stood up. I stepped to the tiny mirror to check my appearance. There were dark circles under my brown eyes, though not as bad as the last time I'd looked in a mirror. My freckles had come out in full force since I'd begun my travels, which made me wrinkle my nose in distaste. Mussed from my nap, my blonde hair frizzed around my face.

In short, the miles I had traveled had written lines of exhaustion on my face.

Shaking my head, I did what I could to bring my hair back into control. What I needed, and wasn't going to get until I reached my father's house, was a long soak in a bath.

Instead, I used the pitcher of water and a rag to remove the dust and sweat from my skin.

For a moment I debated whether I should put on my blue traveling dress, but then I opened my trunk to pull out a lighter green one to wear for the rest of the day. It was slightly wrinkled from its time in the trunk, but it was nice to wear something different. I made quick work of putting my boots on and then I felt ready to face the dining room.

Stew, biscuits, and coffee, the day's specialty, made up my meal. I'd just finished my last bite of stew, which was one of the more tasty meals I'd had since Chicago, when someone sat across from me. The tall, brown-haired man offered a charming smile and leaned his elbows against the table.

"What...pretty girl like you...alone?"

It was not the first time some cowboy tried to charm me while I ate alone. Maybe if I had my hearing and could talk properly I could have sent them all on their way with a flea in their ear.

Offering what I hoped was a polite but disinterested smile, I stood up to pay my bill. The last thing I wanted to do was give any indication of encouragement as men didn't seem to need it to persist in flirting with me.

The man caught my wrist as I tried to walk past. Annoyed, I tried to break free. "Let go!" I said, without really meaning to.

His expression became puzzled just as every other person's face did whenever I spoke. I was aware my voice pitch was unusually high whenever I spoke. Or that's what Aunt Ruth had always told me.

"...wrong with you?" the cowboy asked.

It was a question put to me many times over the years and after my time at school, it only annoyed me further. I managed to wrench away from him, and I continued on my way.

Out of the corner of my eye, I saw the man shadow me as I paid for my meal. I suppose a young woman on her own was seen as good as a soiled dove and available for any man to take advantage of. It wasn't a fair situation as I had no choice in the matter.

The man seemed determined to follow me, so I didn't want to show him where my room was. On the other hand, I was in no mood to go exploring in a strange town.

How I wished I was in Springfield or back at school where I at least knew people who would help me.

Here in the west, until I reached my family, I was on my own.

Taking a deep breath, I stepped outside and walked along the boardwalk. It was mid-afternoon, so there were many people out and about. I hoped that would be enough to discourage my shadow and he would leave me alone.

One of my fellow students had been helpful enough to teach not only me, but all the young ladies at school, how to defend ourselves against someone who wanted to take advantage of us.

We had to be wary of such things. As deaf women, it would be easier for such things to occur, and sadly, they did happen. Some of the younger girls, as soon as they could express themselves, had hair-raising stories that would make any mild-tempered person angry at the world.

I'd not yet had an opportunity to use the knife I had hidden in my boot. Aunt Ruth had been the one to show me that trick when she'd had a long, serious talk about how important it was for a girl to protect her virtue from unscrupulous men.

It had made me more confident as I journeyed to the Montana territory.

Raising my chin, I turned my steps back towards the hotel and didn't stop walking until I was there. No one stopped me along the way, but my heart raced the entire way. When I reached my room and securely locked the door behind me, my hands started to shake. I sat on the edge of the bed before my knees gave way. The adrenaline that had surged through my veins was gone, leaving me shaky and exhausted.

I want to go home, was all I could think. But where was home? The school in Hartford? Or Aunt Ruth's house in Springfield?

To be honest, after two months, I just wasn't as sure as I'd once been. Maybe I would find it in Montana.

A NIGHT OF SLEEP IN a bed put me into a better mood, which I needed given that I was once again faced with being in a stagecoach for hours on end. Though I found myself traveling with five other men, I was fortunate one of them was older and seemed kind in a fatherly way. He put a stop to one of the other passenger's interest in me when he saw how uncomfortable I was.

Thus, my journey continued in as peaceful a manner as was possible. The scenery that we passed became more interesting, and I spent most of my time watching the trees and rocks rush past. It was almost unbearably hot in the coach, though outside the air was milder.

The weather had changed so much. It had been early spring with flowers blooming. I hadn't known what to expect once I left Massachusetts and hadn't been prepared for the heat that hit during several portions of my journey.

I felt the coach jolt as it increased speed. The bouncing became more erratic as I saw the other passengers panicked around me.

What was happening?

The fingers of my right hand gripped the padded seat, and my left clutched at the side of the coach. I dared to glance out the window and regretted it immediately. Keeping pace beside the coach with ease were several horses and riders with handkerchiefs covering the lower halves of their faces.

Stagecoach robbers!

Chapter Two

My heart skipped a beat as I stared at the men. Of course, I'd known there was the risk of this happening when I began, but I had convinced myself that the stories were often exaggerated and travel was as safe as it had ever been.

And now I was in the middle of it with no idea what I should do.

The coach slowed and then came to a stop. As soon as the coach halted, the door was pulled open, and a rifle came into sight. No doubt the owner of said gun barked out an order for us to come out.

Sending a concerned glance in my direction, the kindly man who had looked out for me was the first to climb out. He moved with slow, deliberate actions, his hands in view at all times. The other men followed suit and then it was my turn.

I swallowed hard and leaned down to pick up my slate. Then, as I stepped out, my boot caught on my long skirt, and I pitched forward. Four hands grabbed me before I hit the ground, which I was grateful for until I looked up and discovered that the hands belonged to two of the masked men.

My cheeks burned with embarrassment, overriding any fear I might have had, and, as quick as I could, I joined the other passengers. The kind, silver-haired gentleman stepped to be between the masked men and me. I peered over his shoulder to see what was happening.

That was when I saw that the brave man who rode up with the driver was hunched on the driver's bench. There was no sign of his rifle. Narrowing my eyes, I spotted something bright red where his hand was pressed against his shoulder.

He'd been shot?

Any charity I might have felt over the mannerly way I'd been assisted vanished at that moment. What would drive someone to do this, shooting a man and then rifling through other's belongings? Just for money and then to be on the run from all society? It made no sense!

One by one, the other passengers were "encouraged" to give up any money or valuables on their person. And then, one of the masked men gestured at me. My fingers tightened on my reticule, and the kind gentleman held his arm out as though to create a barrier to keep the man from me.

A rifle came up, and the man was forced to take a step to the side. Raising my chin, I stared at the man as I held out the reticule. He couldn't know that I kept the majority of my funds in my boot. It was a trick I'd learned early on, keeping just enough money in my purse for the day so that if such a thing like a robbery ever happened, a thief would think nothing of it and not search my person any further.

The thief's blue eyes stayed on me as he took my purse. He tossed it to one of his partners and caught my hand. The handkerchief covering his face kept me from seeing whether he spoke, but he must have. He brought my hand up and kissed my fingers through the cloth of his mask.

Swiftly, I pulled my hand away, a shiver running down my spine. His head went back as though he was laughing. My cheeks felt as though they were even more on fire, embarrassed by the attention and being helpless to stop it.

My gaze dropped. While his brown trousers were like any other, same as his red shirt, there was a strange design on the toe of his boots. I had seen leather marked like that before—saddles and saddlebags came to my mind—but I'd never seen boots with a swirling pattern worked into the leather.

Staring at it, I tried to commit it to memory. When we reached the next town, and this holdup was reported, perhaps this small detail would help identify these men. After all, I couldn't describe their voices.

Within a few minutes, the thieves were on their horses and going their way with the money they'd collected and all the guns. The driver jumped to assist the man who had been riding beside him.

One man in a wrinkled business suit threw his hat on the ground and ran his hand through his oily hair. Whatever he had to say on the matter I couldn't see for he turned so that I could not observe. From the way the other men nodded, they agreed with what was said.

My heart refused to slow down, and a tremble had found its way into my fingers. Breathing out, I tried to calm down. It hadn't been as bad as it could have been, that was for sure. I'd been told tales of hold-ups that had resulted in death. Being short a few dollars was hardly anything to cry about in light of how it could have been.

Sooner than I was ready for, the driver was motioning for us to get back in, but then again, I don't think anyone wanted to stay in the area. The driver's partner was put in the coach with the rest of us, and then we were off once again.

Blood was spreading across the bandage being held against the wounded man's injury. I hoped that it wouldn't be far to the next town.

A SHERIFF IN THE SMALL town we came to questioned all the passengers, myself included, which had been a tiresome process. Last I'd been told, the injured man was expected to survive and that it could have been much worse.

It was a relief to put it all behind me. Two days later, I arrived in Colorado City, a day later than I had expected. The moment I stepped off the stage, I couldn't resist sending a quick glance around to see just where I would be living. After all, this was where my father and brother had spent most of the last ten years of their lives. Would I find a home here just as they did?

Before I could take in much beyond the wooden buildings that lined the dusty street, a passenger who was anxious to disembark collided with my back and sent me stumbling forward. I braced myself to meet the boardwalk, but instead, I found myself with my face against a clothed chest. As I sucked my breath in with surprise, I smelled pine, sweat, and the unmistakable scent of horses.

It wasn't unpleasant. In fact, it was preferable to the body odor that had filled the stagecoaches I'd been in for most of my journey. It put me in mind of hard work and was somewhat how I imagined a cowboy would smell like. Not that I'd ever put any thought into how people smelled.

Two hands grabbed my shoulders, helping me to straighten up and regain my balance. I lifted my gaze and again, my breath caught in my throat.

He had to be the most handsome young man I'd ever laid eyes on, and I had traveled over a thousand miles and seen quite a few men. I was close enough to see that freckles dotted his nose, though they were faint. A lock of sandy brown hair was visible under his cowboy hat. His eyes were dark brown and held a mixture of concern and impatience.

Oh, had he said something?

Flustered, I took a step away from him. "Thank you," I said, lifting my right hand to my mouth and making the sign I used most often. Whether anyone could understand me or not, I had to mind my manners.

Like every other person who heard me speak, confusion made his forehead furrow, and he tilted his head slightly. "Are you...right?"

With a quick nod, I tried to compose myself. It wasn't the first time I had run into someone, so why was I unsettled this time? Someone behind me brushed against me and reminded that I was nearly in the street. I took a step to the side so that I would not get in anyone's way.

Would this young man know where I would find my father or brother?

Before I could work out how to ask him, someone moved into view next to him, clapping him on his shoulder. It took only a moment, but I knew him. Here was a younger, taller version of my father. His strawberry blonde hair was like my own, which we had inherited from our mother.

"Simon!" left my lips before I could stop myself. Once upon a time, he'd been my one playmate, patient with me when I first lost my hearing. I'd missed him when he first left, but school had filled my life. Seeing him once again filled me with happiness.

Puzzlement appeared in his hazel eyes, and he frowned. "Do I know... ma'am?" I watched him say.

He didn't recognize me. Of course, how would he? I'd only been six years old when he left but hadn't Aunt Ruth always said I looked exactly like Mama? Had the years made Simon forget what our mother had looked like?

As disturbing as that thought was, I tried not to let it bother me. I'd made sure to put Mama and Father's wedding photograph in the front of the novel I carried with me. I pulled it out and held it out to him. For a moment, he refused to take it, his eyes searching my face. It was only when I made an impatient gesture with the photograph that he took it.

The man who had saved me from hitting the ground also leaned over to have a look. My brother's eyes widened as they moved across the photograph. "No," he said, looking from the photograph to me. He shook his head as if he wanted to deny it all. "Ivy?"

Smiling broadly, I nodded. My brother didn't move to embrace me or give any welcome. He merely continued to stare at me as though I were a ghost, and the photo fell from his hand. I told myself that I had expected this meeting to be awkward, and it was too soon to expect anything different.

The man who had saved me rescued the photograph from the dirt and handed it to me. I tucked it under my arm because I couldn't contain my excitement and my hands needed to move. "I am so happy to see you, Simon," I signed, having to spell out his name with my right hand. I'd never needed to come up with a special sign for him, but I shifted the idea to the back of my mind to give the matter some thought. It would have to be something that fit him just right. "Where is Father?"

"She's deaf?" the stranger beside my brother asked, his eyebrows practically reaching his hat. "Do...know her? Who is she?"

An expression I didn't immediately understand appeared on my brother's face. Was that...shame? "She's my sister," he finally said. He rubbed the back of his neck and refused to look at me.

"You never said you...sister."

Had Simon never talked about me? Yes, ten years was a long time, but there had never been a conversation where he could have mentioned me? I found that hard to believe and it was hard not to feel a little hurt.

"We don't...." I couldn't see the rest of Simon's sentence because he turned away, but I could guess what he said.

They don't talk about me. Because I was deaf? Because as long as I wasn't there, they didn't need to think or make mention of me?

It was apparent, in any event, that my family did not expect me. Shouldn't Uncle Richard have sent a telegram or some notice that I was coming? Perhaps it just hadn't arrived? Or had he simply sent me on my way without a care about what happened to me once I left his house?

The last wasn't so difficult to believe.

To the left, I saw my carpetbag come sailing down from the top of the stagecoach, and it landed by my leg. It was a good thing I didn't have anything breakable in there. The hand mirror I'd packed carefully in my trunk, which, when I looked over my shoulder, was in the process of being brought down for me.

Simon and his friend were still talking, my brother's body language becoming more and more defensive. What was being said? I reached out and touched Simon's arm to get his attention. He faced me with a start.

"Father?" I mouthed, not trusting myself to use my voice again. I held up one finger and moved it from side to side like I would search a map for a location. "Where?"

My brother's shoulders rose and fell with a sigh. He bent over and picked up my carpet bag. "See you," I saw him say before he turned.

I offered the young man a smile before I hurried after Simon and he gave me a brief nod of acknowledgment. There would time enough for introductions later. I hoped.

Simon's steps were fast, almost like he wished he could outrun me. I suppose to have a sister one was ashamed of showing up out of nowhere, with no warning, would put anyone in a bad mood. He could have been a little more considerate about it, though.

Four blocks from where the stagecoach had stopped, I saw my family's store for the first time. The sign, Steele General Store, was not as lovely as the sign in Springfield, but it gave me a sense of home to see it. There were several differences between the store Aunt Ruth and Father had been joint owners of in Springfield and the one here in Montana, mostly in the materials of the structure.

Without slowing his steps at all, Simon charged into the building and didn't give me much time to study the outside or to get an idea of what was displayed in the windows. No one was browsing the shelves, which was preferable for a family meeting. How would Father react to seeing me?

An unfamiliar young woman, her black hair in a long braid that rested on her shoulder, was behind the counter. She was taller than me by about six inches, which made me feel even smaller than usual. "What...wrong, Si?" she asked, her gaze curiously flicking over me. Did she just call my brother, "Si"?

With Simon's back to me, I couldn't see what he said, but I could see the change of emotions of her face. Her eyes widened, and she shook her head. "What? You're joking."

By this point, I was tired of watching people express their shock and surprise at my appearance. Was it extraordinary for someone to return to their family after such a long time apart? But, no. I couldn't forget that apparently, no one in this town knew about me, so I suppose it would be a surprise to everyone.

Forcing a smile, I stepped forward to stand next to my brother and held my gloved hand out to her. As soon as I crossed the Mississippi, I'd learned quickly that this was the typical way of greeting people. The young woman just stared at me with brown eyes full of suspicion, and I self-consciously pulled my hand back.

"Your father…in…back," she said, moving her gaze back to Simon. "I'll–"

Her offer to get Father, which was what I guessed she had been about to say, was cut off by something Simon said. My brother dropped my carpet bag on the floor and stepped around the counter. He vanished through the doorway, and I remained where I was.

The young woman flipped her braid over her shoulder and came out from behind the counter. In a manner that hinted she was ignoring me, she walked to the front of the store. I twisted around to watch her. She flipped over a sign that indicated the shop was closed and shut the door. Instead of returning to the counter, she walked down one of the aisles, out of my sight.

Nervousness made me flex my fingers. This was not how I expected this to go. I wasn't sure what I expected, but this upset was not it.

I saw movement out of the corner of my eye, and I turned back. For the first time in ten years, my father was in front of me, and he looked better than I remembered. No longer was he ill from the infection in the wound that had sent him home from the war. The beard he'd had the last time I saw him, that had graced his face for his wedding photograph, and that was in all of my memories, was gone.

There was no getting around that he stared at me as though I were a ghost. "Ivy." That was all he said as he came toward me. His brown eyes, which Simon and I had inherited from him, were bright with emotion. Then, his arms came around me, and my face was pressed against his vest as he embraced me tightly.

At that moment, I was exactly where I wanted to be.

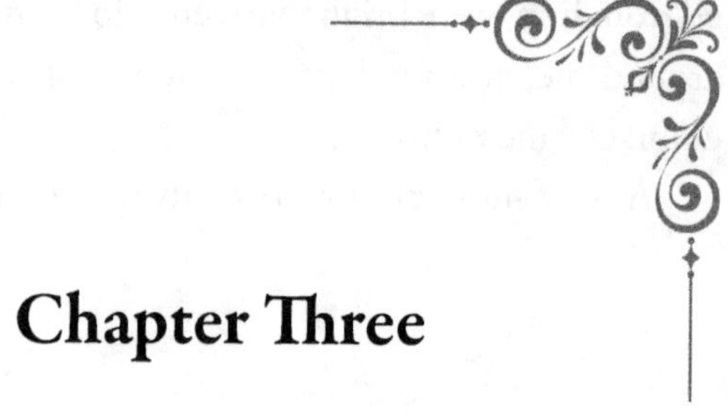

Chapter Three

All too soon, Father released me and stepped back. He cupped my cheek with his left hand and stared at me like he wanted to remember every detail of my face. Pulling his hand back, he turned toward the counter. He pulled a pad of paper from somewhere and began to write. His immediate desire to communicate with me warmed my heart.

I took the opportunity to study him. His appearance hadn't changed much. He was still tall, though not as tall as I remembered since my six-year-old mind had considered him next to a giant. There were more lines around his face, and there was an air of seriousness around him that made me sad. He'd smiled so much before the war.

He'd also gained some weight. He'd been frail when he was discharged from the army. An infection had taken its toll on him, although it hadn't necessitated the removal of his arm. He was dressed in a suit and vest, appropriate attire for a storekeeper.

As I waited to read whatever he was writing, I glanced over my shoulder. Simon was deep in conversation with the young woman, who was looking more and more upset. A hand on my arm made me refocus on my father, who handed me the paper.

It took several seconds for me to decipher his handwriting. He'd been right-handed before the injury during battle made his right arm useless. Now, though he had taught himself how to write with his left hand, the letters were shaky and badly formed.

Ivy, what are you doing here? Is Ruth with you?

He didn't know about Aunt Ruth's death. Oh, why hadn't Uncle Richard sent word? Father was Aunt Ruth's only brother. A telegram should have been sent with the news. Now I had to be the one to tell him.

Taking a deep breath, I stepped to the counter and set down my reticule. As I picked up the pen, the memories made my eyes fill with tears.

I remembered knowing that I was too late to help Aunt Ruth. Desperation had sent me running for the doctor. There were details I couldn't bring myself to share: how I'd tripped over my skirt when I rushed to the door and ran down the street to the doctor's house.

To write that the doctor had covered Aunt Ruth's body with a blanket was a cold, emotionless way of describing what had happened the scene. I couldn't explain my anxiety and grief as the policemen tried to question me before they were informed I was deaf.

How could I explain Uncle Richard's attitude when he walked on the scene? That he'd immediately blamed me? A part of me wondered whether my uncle was right on that point. If I'd had my hearing, would I have heard Aunt Ruth call for help?

In the end, I wrote two sentences. *Aunt Ruth is dead. Uncle Richard sent me to you.*

There would be time enough for more explanations later.

Father read my words, the frown furrowing his forehead going deeper and deeper. When he finished, he shook his head and covered his face with his left hand. When he dropped his hand, he handed my note to Simon.

"Poor girl," I saw Father say as he lifted his head. Grief was written on his face, and I felt awful at having to give him the news in such a way. He blinked rapidly, his eyes shining bright with tears. "What have you been through?"

A great deal, but I had no desire to add to his grief. I forced a smile.

Reaching out, Father hugged me once again with his good arm. I felt the rise and fall of his breathing with my head against his chest. It was amazing how comforted I felt.

After just a few moments, I was released once more, and Father was in motion. He collected his hat and coat from the back. Hefting my carpet bag with his uninjured hand, he led the way out of the store.

He gave several commands to Simon and the woman as he went out, one of which was for them to lock up. On the sidewalk, he set off to the right, walking away from the main part of the small town. I kept pace beside him, trying to take everything in.

There was a freshness in the air, with undertones of pine and cattle. Men on horses tipped their hats as they went by, just as cowboys in other towns had done. Ladies inclined their heads, pausing in their conversation to greet my father. I garnered curious glances with every step I took.

The last house before the town officially ended was where Father left the road. It was much smaller than Aunt

Ruth's brick house in Springfield and made only of wood. There was a lovely flowerbed along the porch and a white-washed fence around it.

As Father opened the gate, the front door of the house opened. A brown-haired child in a blue dress came running out, bare feet flying on the wood porch. There was a delighted grin on her face as she went down the steps.

"Papa! Papa!" her lips said as she clapped her hands together.

Dropping my bag, Father knelt down and caught the child in a hug, his head tilted back with a laugh. How I remembered greeting him in such a manner when I was little more than a toddler! But who was this?

I knew he had remarried four years ago, but his letters had never mentioned I had a new sibling.

The girl noticed me and pointed in my direction. Father turned and said, "Katie girl, this...Ivy."

Forcing a smile, I crouched and held my hand out. Little Katie scowled at me, her brown eyes—so like Simon's—filled with suspicion. The young woman from the store pushed past me, nearly knocking me off balance, and swept Katie out of Father's arms. She continued on her way into the house.

Why was she here? Did the woman Father marry have children of her own? Did I have step-siblings?

The idea both excited me and made me nervous as I straightened up. My friends at school had always referred to their siblings with affection and exasperation. I'd been too young to have that kind of relationship with Simon, and I'd been looking forward to forming such with him. A sister, who I could share ideas about clothes would be fun, but we hadn't gotten off on the right foot.

I followed Father into the house and immediately breathed in the heavenly scent of baking bread. The morning errands I'd done in Springfield had taken me past bakeries, but they had nothing on the smell in that house. My mouth watered in anticipation.

A woman, who looked enough like the young woman from the store to tell me they were related, came from the back of the house. She frowned at me, trying to calm the toddler on her hip.

"Peter, what...this Anna has told me about...daughter?"

So not only did I have at least one stepsister named Anna, I had two half-siblings and a third on the way, judging by the rounded belly of the woman. What had Father's letter said her name was? Cordelia?

With Father facing away from me, I wasn't able to see what he said. Instead, I smiled at the toddler, who was staring at me with open interest. I wiggled my fingers at the child—the shapeless white gown did not indicate the gender—and earned a smile in response.

When I refocused on Cordelia, her expression was one of outrage. "How? We barely...room for our own....," she said, shifting her toddler to her other hip. "Why didn't you tell me?"

Why hadn't Father told his new bride he had a daughter? Or had he told her but not mentioned the fact that I was deaf? No doubt he hadn't expected me to ever come to the Montana territory.

My father stepped to her and leaned close to her ear. I noticed Anna stood in the doorway, interested in the conversation. When Father stepped back, Cordelia did not appear appeased but more resigned.

"How do I even talk to her?" she asked.

That seemed as good a time as any to step forward. "Hello. I'm Ivy," I said, spelling my name out and then showing my sign name. I'd given it to myself soon after I went to school. Holding my pinkie up, I made a zigzag pattern in the air, like how an ivy plant grows. "I am pleased to meet you."

Some of my classmates had their names given to them, and the rest, like me, made their own. One of the ways we'd spent our evenings had been in devising interesting and unique ways to sign names. A person's personality had a lot to do with it.

Cordelia frowned. "What is she doing?"

Father glanced back at me as I tried not to feel hurt. I'd hoped my family would at least learn a few signs to communicate with me, as Aunt Ruth and the reverend's wife back home had done. Life was going to be complicated if they didn't.

"Ivy uses her hands to speak," Father said, making sure he kept his face towards me even though he was talking to his wife. He remembered! In my letters, I had mentioned how difficult it could be to carry on conversations when people looked away. "She reads lips."

That bit of information didn't seem to appease my stepmother at all. She spun around and vanished back where I assumed the kitchen was located.

As far as first meetings went, it could have gone better, but it also could have been much worse. Hopefully, with time, we could find some common ground.

Dinner was, predictably, awkward for us all. Simon didn't make eye contact with me through the whole meal, and neither did Anna. My stepsister had talked the entire time, though, her head turned away just enough so that I couldn't read her lips. My second stepsister—Susan—kept glancing at my but otherwise kept her head down.

And I'd thought meals with Uncle Richard had been difficult!

Father, as often as he could, tried to at least address a statement to me every few minutes. He had ensured I sat next to him, which had annoyed the rest of the family. Now and then, he reached over to squeeze my hand.

The food—a stew and the bread I had smelled as soon as I entered the house—was excellent. If nothing else, I enjoyed that part of the experience.

It was after the meal that the real awkwardness began. Ordering her daughters to do the dishes, Cordelia sat next to Father on the delicate settee that was the absolute opposite of anything a man would have chosen for his home. I guessed my stepmother must have brought it with her when she married Father. The question I had been waiting for was finally asked.

"Why aren't you at school?"

The beginning of my explanation, both with miming and writing, that the money had not been available for another year sent Father into a rage. I gathered from the words he exchanged with his wife that while money was tight and he'd written to say there would be a slight delay before the funds for my tuition and board, he had every intention of me continuing my education.

Why had Aunt Ruth said there was no money for me to continue at school? Had there been some miscommunication?

If that was true, would I be able to return? I tried in vain to rein in my excitement at the idea. It had been a small fortune for me to travel all the way to Montana, but I was certainly not a welcome addition to the family.

Cordelia pursed her lips, and I wondered if she'd been aware of the money Father had spent on my education. It was hard to believe that she hadn't noticed, but if she wasn't aware of me, what excuse had Father given her about the money?

"Richard wouldn't allow you to stay with him?" was the next question put to me.

I gave a nod, remembering those black and white words Uncle Richard had written just hours after I found Aunt Ruth dead. *Ivy, you will leave this house.* A mere five days later, the day after Aunt Ruth was buried, I was on my way to the Montana territory.

In the time it took me to explain it all, Anna and Susan had finished cleaning up and they put the toddlers to bed as well. There was no sign of Simon. Why hadn't he wanted to know how I'd come to be in the Montana territory? Had the years created a permanent wedge between us?

Glancing up, I was surprised to see open horror on my stepmother's face. She covered her mouth as she said something to Father. The dismay and horror that appeared in his expression confused me. What had she said?

Color crept his neck, and he tugged at the collar of his shirt. He was slow to write his next question and scratched out several words after he wrote them. Then, he refused to look at me when he handed it over.

Were you unmolested on your journey?

Appalled by the question, I felt a blush spread across my cheeks. I wrote an emphatic: *Yes!* Why would Cordelia have suggested such a thing? Was she searching for a reason to turn me out? I knew such things happen when a young lady was less than completely respectable.

Relief filled Father's face as he read my answer, and he nodded. Cordelia, though, looked unconvinced and again, she covered her mouth to speak to my father. She'd picked up on that method of keeping her words from me far too quickly for my comfort.

"You would tell me, wouldn't you?"

That he'd even had to ask made me sigh, and the growing relief on his face when I gave a nod was disheartening. I tried to tell myself the time we'd been apart meant he wouldn't know me. How could he?

Still, reliving the painful memories on top of the long day I'd spent on the stagecoach was catching up with me. Fatigue made my eyelids heavy, and I fought to keep from yawning.

Father must have seen it for he collected all the papers as he stood up. "Let you...sleep. Anna."

Rolling her eyes, Anna secured her needle in the piece of fabric she'd been working on. She placed her needlework in a basket and rose from the rocking chair. Guessing she was my guide to where I would sleep, I followed her up the stairs to the second floor.

It was a relief to retreat and escape Cordelia's scrutiny. However, when I was in a small bedroom, I was in for another surprise. Anna pointed to where an already sleeping Katie was occupying most of the bed.

Granted, I had shared a bed when I was younger, but that was years in my past. I didn't know this child. What if she woke in the night and was frightened by a stranger? Why didn't Anna sleep with the sister she'd known from birth? Or why couldn't she and I share the bed while the younger Susan, thirteen years old if I'd understood my father correctly, shared with Katie? It would make more sense than to put the toddler with me.

Undoubtedly there was a chair or a couch I could sleep on until something else could be arranged. When I turned to protest, though, Anna was already gone.

Exhausted and with no energy to go in search of my step-sister, I crawled onto the bed. Morning would be time enough to suggest a change.

Chapter Four

In the middle of the night, warm wetness on my side pulled me from my sleep. As I breathed in, the pungent scent of urine filled my nostrils, and it took all my willpower not to gag. Beside me, little Katie slept on, blissfully unaware that she had wet the bed.

Feeling more than a little sorry for myself, I stared up at the dark ceiling. Sharing a bed with a three-year-old with no bladder control was not how I had envisioned the first night with my family.

Moving as close to the edge as possible, I tried to go back to sleep. By the time dawn broke, though, I didn't feel rested at all. Besides wetting the bed, Katie was a kicker and several times, just as I was drifting to sleep, I would be startled awake by a foot connecting with my ribs.

At least I didn't have the complaint of snores keeping me awake.

It was Sunday, which I realized when Father had reminded everyone the night before that he would not wait to leave for the church if there were any sluggards in the morning. Maybe he'd said it for my benefit so that I would know the family routine.

The smell of urine followed me as I stood up and pulled my nightgown off. I tried to move as quietly as I could so I wouldn't wake the others. Thus, it took longer for me to get dressed. My trunk had been left downstairs, so I was left with the travel wrinkled gowns I'd kept in my bag. I felt fortunate that I did have one, a gray cotton with pale pink flowers embroidered, that would be serviceable for church.

I climbed down the stairs and headed for to the outhouse in the back. Quick to finish my business, I stepped out into the growing light. For a moment, I stood in the dewy grass and stared at the horizon. Perhaps after some time in the territory, I would get used to the pine scent and the magnificent mountains that touched the sky, but not just yet.

There was a slight chill in the air, and I shivered, rubbing my arms to warm them. I hurried back to the house. The kitchen was lit from within, and I guessed that Cordelia had begun breakfast.

The woman was stirring the contents of a bowl near the stove when I entered. In order not to startle her, I rapped my knuckles against the doorframe. She glanced over her shoulder, and the corners of her mouth turned downward immediately. I tried not to be hurt be her immediate displeasure. After all, she hadn't expected a step-daughter from the east to arrive on her doorstep with no warning.

"Can I help?" I signed. I had no desire to be treated as a guest and could pull my own weight. Too late did I realize that she wouldn't understand me.

"What?" she asked, a frown creasing her forehead.

Moving forward, I held out my hands to take the bowl from her. She stepped back, her hands tightening on it. Startled, I stared at her, struggling to understand why she would be so defensive. I only wanted to help, not take over her kitchen.

"What do...want?" she asked.

I fisted my left hand, placed it on top of my right palm, and raised them. "To help you," I said at the same time. I'd managed to teach Aunt Ruth signs in a similar manner. Hopefully, Cordelia and the rest of my family would eventually pick up on what I meant.

She shook her head and turned her back on me. Unsure what to do, I watched as she spooned the batter onto the griddle. The scent of pancakes filled the air a few moments later, and Cordelia continued to ignore my presence in the kitchen.

Frustrated, I took a step back, resisting the urge to retreat. It was like being back in Springfield and being under Uncle Richard's criticism again, only now I was in a strange home with no idea about the routine. There had to be some way for me to help. Maybe...maybe I could set the table?

Cordelia had the plates stacked on the edge of the counter. I took a deep breath and went to her side. I picked them up, but out of the corner of my eye, I saw Cordelia turn towards me. In an instant, she was next to me, her hand curling around my left wrist. She jerked me around to face her.

"What are you doing?" Her vehemence in her expression took me even more aback.

"Helping," I said, aloud as my hands were full of plates. At least by now, she'd stopped flinching whenever I used my voice.

"Get out."

For a moment, I wondered if I'd read her lips right. Why was she so offended by my offer to help? Was it because her daughter was still asleep and not there to help her? Or was it I was her husband's daughter, a reminder that he'd had love before her? But, as far as I could tell, she'd not shown any antagonism towards Simon. Was it because she didn't know me? Did she not like strangers?

Firmly, Cordelia pulled the plates away from me as these questions ran through my mind. She slammed them down on the counter and returned to her cooking. This time, I did retreat, trying desperately not to cry. Father was in the parlor, an open book in his left hand. He looked up as I came in and a frown appeared on his face. Something of my emotions must have been on my face.

"What...wrong?" he asked.

Would telling him just make things worse? I had the feeling it would, so I shook my head. He held his hand out, and I went to him. I sat on the arm of the chair, and he put his good arm around me. It was comforting to be beside him, and I tried to read the book he had in his other hand.

Though it was not one I had seen before, several of the boys at school had made mention of it: *Twenty Thousand Leagues Under the Sea* by Jules Verne. He was in the middle of the book, so I had little idea what the plot was. I made a mental note to ask to read it whenever he finished.

We remained like that until Simon came down, blurry-eyed and scruffy-faced. He vanished outside, and I hoped he would return looking more presentable. It wasn't many minutes later until Anna entered. She sent a scowl in my direction before rushing to the kitchen. A moment later, she was back and going up to the second floor.

Father closed his book and stood up. He went to the table, which was laden with food, and took his seat at the head. I surmised that Cordelia had called out that breakfast was ready, for my siblings came rushing to the table not a minute later. Susan was barely dressed, and Katie was still in her nightgown. Simon had, while he was outside, shaved and looked more awake than before.

Breakfast was no less awkward than the evening meal had been. Cordelia again covered her mouth as she spoke to my Father. This time Father merely shook his head at her and made some comment about how the weather would be beautiful. Whatever complaint she had against me, whether for trying to help or something else, would have to wait.

There were seven of us around the table, and the baby sat on Cordelia's knee. As soon as the last scrap of food was eaten, Susan and Anna began collecting the dishes. I jumped up to help, but they both snatched up every plate I reached for. They couldn't enjoy washing dishes so much they didn't want my help, could they?

In the corner, I could see Father and Cordelia having an intense discussion. Simon watched them and then threw a glance in my direction. It was a conversation about me, apparently. That wasn't a surprise at all.

With nothing to do and some time until it was time to leave for church, I went up to the attic. What was I supposed to do with the urine soaked sheets and blankets? There wouldn't be time to wash them before church. Still, I stripped the bed and made a pile at the foot of the bed. Maybe after we returned, I could take care of it.

The scent of urine still clung to the air as I sat on the edge of the bed. I pulled my brush from my carpet bag and set about arranging my hair into something more than a quick braid. The bath I'd been hoping for once I arrived in Colorado City hadn't happened yet, so I did the best I could.

Before long, Anna and Susan came up to change. The young woman, who I thought was close to my age, stepped up to me and poked me with her finger. "...you're special because you...from the East?" she said, her face close to mine.

"What?" My hands moved out of habit. I had been in Colorado City for less than twenty-four hours. How could she jump to that absurd conclusion in so short a time?

She wrinkled her nose as she stepped back. She made a gesture with her right hand. "That...weird. Stop..."

My signing was weird? Annoyance surged past my confusion. Deliberately, I lifted my hands and began to sign. *"This is how I communicate with the world, and I'm not going to stop because you don't like it."*

Her scowl returning, Anna spun and went to the other side of the attic, which wasn't far. Susan stared at me with brown eyes wide with curiosity. When she realized her sister had turned away, she did so as well, though she would glance over her shoulder every few seconds to see what I was doing.

I focused on smoothing and twisting my hair into a low knot at the base of my neck. In my travels, I'd gotten skilled at doing it without the benefit of a mirror. I slid the hairpins into place, securing the chignon. It would take a force of nature, like a strong wind, to dislodge it.

Leaving my two stepsisters to finish dressing, I went downstairs. As I walked around the small house, avoiding the closed door that led to Father and Cordelia's bedroom, I marveled at how few furnishings and decorations there were. Beyond the curtains and the settee, there were no apparent signs that a woman lived there.

Either they had not been there long, or they were in the process of leaving.

As I ran my finger along the fireplace mantel, Simon entered. He tugged on the tie around his neck as he glanced at his reflection in the window. Apparently satisfied with how he looked, he turned and raised his eyebrow at me.

I lifted my hand in greeting. Without saying a word, he left the parlor and went outside. Every hope I'd had of a bond with my only brother shattered right then. Why did he treat me as though I were a complete stranger?

Yes, ten years was a long time, but we'd had six, almost seven, years growing up together. We'd played together, studied together, and grieved together. It had broken my heart when Father took Simon with him, and the expression on my brother's face when he looked back at me from the carriage that had taken him away had been filled with sadness.

Father, adjusting his collar, came into the room. He barely glanced at me as he called out for everyone to hurry up. It was time to walk to the church.

ARM IN ARM, FATHER and Cordelia led the way. My stepmother had her toddler, Sam, on her right hip. Katie was next, holding Susan's hand. Anna was next to me, ignoring me with every step she took, and then Simon was behind us.

To be quite honest, it was the strangest walk to church I had ever been a part of. At school, there had been a chapel on school grounds, and the reverend had delivered his sermon in sign for us. In Springfield, I had always trailed behind my aunt and uncle. To be in the center of a group was disconcerting.

There was already a large group milling about the yard of the white church. I took a deep breath, drawing on all my courage. Meeting new people had become a bit easier since I'd set out for Montana, but it still was not my favorite thing to do.

Father pulled his arm away from Cordelia and turned to reach his good hand out to me. Stepping around Katie, I went to him. He kept me by his side as he approached the closest man. They shook hands, exchanging greetings. My eyes went to the badge on his vest.

"Miss," he said, tipping his hat to me. "Welcome to town."

"—my daughter Ivy," Father said, making sure he looked straight at me as he made the introduction though I missed the first part of his sentence. "Ivy, this...Sheriff John Worth."

I nodded in acknowledgment. Father turned back to the sheriff and, I presumed, explained that I was deaf. The sheriff did a double take, looking at me a little closer the second time. I took the opportunity to study him closer. He was of average height, taller than me at least, and had a graying mustache over his lip.

As Father continued to talk to Sheriff Worth, I glanced around. Anna had found several of her friends and was gesturing dramatically as she spoke. They all glanced my way, and then their shoulders shook with laughter. What was she telling them?

A touch on my arm brought my focus back to Father and the sheriff. Sheriff Worth said, with exaggerated mouth movements, "You were on the stage that was held up?"

It would have been comical if it didn't help me understand. I gave a brief nod in answer. Sheriff glanced at Father, who looked concerned. "I received a wire with the news," he said, without the exaggerated speaking. "There...mention of...deaf passenger."

Someone who passed behind the sheriff caught my attention. It was the young man who had caught me! He nodded and tipped his hat when his gaze met mine. A blush heated up my cheeks as I smiled at him. When would I know his name?

All too soon, it was time to enter the church, and I hadn't even met the reverend. While I'd hoped to sit near my father for the service, I was squished in between Simon and Anna. Neither of them looked happy about the situation.

We were in the back pew, so it was impossible for me to see the reverend speak. Out of respect, I stood for the hymns and read along from the hymnal that Anna held in her hands. I didn't even attempt to join my voice with the congregation. That would have been a disaster given that I had little control over volume and pitch.

There was little to occupy my mind as I sat through the sermon. The walls were wooden planks, and the windows were simple. In Springfield, stained glass windows had sparkled and held my attention whenever Uncle Richard sat us too far from the pulpit for me to read Reverend Weston's lips. Here, I was bored out of my mind.

Anna jabbed me in the ribs with her elbow when everyone bowed their heads for the final prayer. When I tried to step away from her, I knocked into Simon, and he too elbowed me in the side. I glared at him, but he had his head down and his eyes closed.

It wasn't always going to be like this, was it?

Chapter Five

I had the feeling that Father and Cordelia noticed the little spat between the three of us. They were quick to lead us out of the church as soon as the service was over. There was no stopping to talk to their neighbors, and we made the short walk to the house much faster than we had earlier in the morning.

It was even more confusing when Cordelia set down bread and ham on the table. She didn't even pause to eat but rushed into her bedroom. Anna pushed Katie towards me and fed Sam. Father took pity on me as I stared at the three-year-old with no idea what I was supposed to do with her. He sat the girl on his knee and shared his food with her.

This was not what I thought being part of a large family would be like.

Everyone ate quickly. Simon was the first to finish, and he rushed out of the room. Was something happening that I didn't know about? Father moved to the chair in front of the fireplace, where he took Katie and Sam onto his lap and began to read to them.

Anna and Susan both vanished into Father and Cordelia's bedroom. Simon entered the house with a small crate in his arms and carried it to the same room. Was Father keeping the toddlers occupied while something else happened?

To remain out of the way, and hoping someone would tell me if there was some task I could help with, I retreated to the bedroom I'd shared the night before. I could smell urine as soon as I opened the door. If it were any other day, I would start the bedclothes soaking, but it was Sunday, the day of rest.

Sittin on the floor by the open window, I opened the book I had carried with me across the country. Time. We all needed time to adjust to me being part of the family.

THE FOLLOWING MORNING, I was greeted by the same rush of activity. Anna was the one in the kitchen. While the day before, she had worn her best dress, today she wore what had to be her oldest dress. The gingham pattern was worn and faded from multiple washings.

My stepsister refused my offer of help, preferring to rush food from the stove to the table. Cordelia came out, dressed in a worn cotton gown. Whatever she said made Anna and Susan rush even more.

Breakfast was simple, and no one spoke as they ate. As soon as Father stood up, Susan began grabbing dishes from the table. Carrying Sam, Father hurried to the bedroom. Standing behind the chair where I had sat for the brief meal, I watched in confusion. Cordelia faced me, and her expression was filled with impatience. She waved her hands in a shooing motion as though she wanted me out of the room.

With no other choice, and completely baffled, I retreated to the parlor. Through the window, I saw a wagon pull up in front of the house. My rescuer from the previous day set the brake and then jumped to the ground. He pushed his hat back as he stared at the house. His expression seemed serious.

I stepped to the side, hoping he hadn't seen me. As I did, I saw Simon rush past the parlor doorway, presumably to meet his friend. My brother had changed out of his suit into trousers and a ragged shirt.

Whatever my family had planned for the afternoon, they expected to get dirty. I needed to know what was happening. As soon as Father came out, dressed in a similar manner as Simon, I hurried to him and wiggled my hands in question. "What is going on?"

For a moment, he stared at me with a frown, and then he glanced around. His shoulders rose and fell with a sigh, and he shook his head. Gesturing for me to follow, Father went to the desk in the parlor and found the only sheet of paper there. He wrote a quick note.

Ivy, I am so sorry we did not tell you. Today, we are moving to the ranch.

Since when did Father own a ranch? He was a store owner! What did he know about ranching? My confusion must have been evident because Father laughed. He took back the paper, wrote some more, and then put it in my hand. He hurried on his way, leaving me to read the note.

There will be more room on the ranch. It's a good move for the future of this family. You'll understand when you see it.

So, none of my questions were answered. Well, I had an answer to two questions. Now I knew why my trunk had been left on the porch. What was the point of carrying it in if it would just have to be brought back out? I also understood why the house looked so bare.

When I looked up, I realized that I wasn't alone in the room. A blush spread on my cheeks once again as the young man, his hat in his hand, nodded at me. Feeling shy, I raised my hand in greeting. Would I learn his name at last? It was strange to think of him as "my rescuer," or the "young man."

"Hello," he said.

Simon stepped around him and glanced between us. He shook his head and made a gesture to his friend. "—Prater, my sister Ivy," he said, looking impatient. "Come help with the furniture." Without waiting for an answer, my brother left the room.

"Pleasure to meet you, Miss Ivy," the young man—I assumed that Prater was his last name— said, putting his hat back on. I'd missed whatever first name my brother had given. I think it ended with 'emy,' which made no sense at all. The only name I knew of that would contain those letters was "Emmy." It was a girl's name, so that couldn't be right.

He waited until I gave a nod of acknowledgment and then he backed out of the room. I could have offered him the paper and gotten his full name. Even though I wanted to know his first name, I was a little glad I hadn't done that. It would have emphasized how different I was, and that was the last thing I ever wanted to do.

I'd known men who'd fought in the war, who now had no leg or arm. While they were treated with care and unease at first, in time they returned to their lives, more or less. But with me...I was always on the outside, looking in.

Shaking my head, I folded up the paper and slipped it into my pocket. It still had room for other writing, and it would have been wasteful to throw it out. After a glance down at my good dress, and not wanting it to be ruined with hard work, I climbed up the ladder to the attic. Anna was already there, scowling at the pile of soiled items at the foot of my bed. She nudged at it with her foot as though she hadn't seen it earlier.

As soon as she saw me, she turned and set about stripping the rest of the beds. Holding back a sigh, I placed my carpet bag on the bed and opened it. I pulled out the second dress that I'd worn on my journey. It was in sore need of a wash, but I assumed that until the entire family was moved to this ranch, I would have no access to a washtub for my clothes or myself. It would have to do, though, for I was not about to put my traveling dress back on.

Anna left the attic with the other bedding while I changed. I made sure all of my belongings were in my bag and then gathered up the soiled sheets. I could only hope that there would be someplace I could store them in the wagon that no one would notice the smell.

More people and wagons had arrived when I climbed down to the main floor. Feeling as though I were in the way, I hurried outside and, after stuffing the bedding in under some of the dining table chairs, I retreated to the porch. At least ten men carried furniture in and out, loading the items onto three different wagons.

Within two hours, the house had been emptied. Sadly, Cordelia had discovered the soiled sheets, and she sent a scowl in my direction as though it were my fault the three-year-old had wet the bed. She allowed them to remain where they were, no doubt not wanting to draw attention to them.

When it was clear there was nothing more to be added, Father helped me up onto one of the wagon seats, and he climbed up to take the reins. That earned me yet another frown from Cordelia, who rightly expected to be by her husband. To make room for her, I climbed over the seat and settled among odds and ends. It wasn't the most comfortable place, but Cordelia was able to sit next to Father with Katie beside her and Sam on her lap.

It was quite a caravan that set off out of town. The sun shone down on us, and most of the group looked happy with the excellent weather. A gentle breeze stirred the tall grass, ensuring that it did not become overbearingly hot. When I glanced at the other wagons, everyone seemed as though they were laughing and talking.

Simon and Mr. Prater were in the wagon behind us, and Anna leaned forward between them. I couldn't be surprised that Anna knew Simon's friend, but it seemed as though she were far closer than I'd ever seen a young lady be with a man. At least, the way she hung on his shoulder didn't seem entirely appropriate.

Unable to watch, I instead turned my thoughts in another direction. How long had this move been expected? Had Father ever mentioned he wished to take up ranching in his letters? Not that I could remember, but perhaps he had mentioned it in one of his letters to Aunt Ruth. Maybe this was why he'd delayed in sending the money for my education.

In the distance, the mountains looked majestic against the blue sky. It was as breathtaking as the view had been earlier that day. The scenery was so different from what I'd known in Springfield and at school. I couldn't get enough of it as I looked around.

It was well over an hour's drive to the ranch house. Several times I nearly dozed off, but a jolt always startled me wide awake. We passed under a sign, which was hanging by one hook, proclaiming it to be the Lazy M ranch.

From the outside, the house appeared bigger than the white house in town. This one had a more rugged look, the sides being log and chink. There was a porch that stretched the entire front, and four windows with glass graced the front as well. Spindly rose bushes with tiny red buds grew by the steps, giving the structure a homey feel.

As soon as the wagon came to a stop, I crawled over some chairs to get to the side and jumped down without any help. Did Father intend for us all to live this far from town? It seemed so unreal.

Everyone else had gone to work unloading the wagons. I had no idea where Cordelia would want things, so I walked up onto the porch. Two rocking chairs were already in place, but whether they had been left there or had been brought at an earlier time was unclear. They faced the mountains at the perfect angle to observe them in all their glory.

Determined to know my new home, I crossed the threshold. I stepped immediately into the main living space, a fireplace to my right and the kitchen directly across from me. To my left were two doors, presumably leading to two bedrooms.

A ladder in between those two doors led to the loft, and I climbed up. Once I was up there, I was able to stand up straight. There was more room there than in the other house, and there was already a sheet dividing the space. Simon would have some privacy from the girls.

Would that mean the youngest children would sleep in the second downstairs bedroom? I hoped so, if only because that meant that I wouldn't have to share my bed.

With a sigh, I turned to the ladder. If I didn't at least offer to help, I knew it would be held against me.

JUST BEFORE THE SUN completely set, the last neighbor set off in his wagon. I'd managed to catch the names of two of them, Mr. Murphy and Mr. Johnson. With so much going on, it had been hard to keep track of what anyone said. By the end of the day, I had a massive headache, and my eyes were tired from the strain.

The interior of the house was chaos, with nothing where it should be. Only the table and chairs were where they would stay, in the center of the kitchen. A single lamp rested in the middle of the table, and a basket of food, left by one of the neighbor ladies, served as our dinner.

As soon as every scrap of food had been consumed, by unanimous agreement, everyone went to their beds. Katie and Sam were put on a small trundle bed in the smaller of the two downstairs bedrooms, just as I had suspected would happen. The rest of us, save for Father and Cordelia, went to the loft.

Frames for the beds had not been put together, so our mattresses were on the floor. Simon retreated behind his curtain without a word to any of us. Susan glanced between my bed and her sister's which was on the other side of the loft. Despite the sharp looks that Anna gave her, the thirteen-year-old plopped herself down opposite me.

Rolling her eyes, Anna made no further protest. She picked up the only candle that had been brought up with us and blew the tiny flame out. I hadn't finished undressing, so being plunged into darkness was particularly irritating. I counted to ten to keep my anger under control.

In fewer than two days, Anna had next to declared war on me. Why? What had I done, besides just arriving, to make her so opposed to me?

At least I'd had my nightgown in my hand, and I pulled it over my hand. Then, I felt my way onto my bed. The slightest scent of urine that still clung to the mattress. Wrinkling my nose, I crawled under the quilt. At least it wasn't wet still.

Would Father send me back to school? I wondered that as I stared up at the dark ceiling. In a month or two, he could send me back, pleased to have seen me but relieved to get back to his new family. And me? I could pursue my goal of teaching at the school.

The more I thought about it, the more it appealed to me. I would be back with those who understood me, who knew the struggles I faced every day, who had never made me feel inferior. I had given it up as a lost cause when Aunt Ruth had broken the news to me.

How could I tactfully make the suggestion? I didn't want Father to think I wasn't happy to see him. I was, however, it was clear that I wasn't welcome by the rest of the family. Not even my only brother wanted me there.

With a sigh, I rolled onto my side. My mind went to the kindness I had seen in those who had helped my family move. It was a trait I had seen in many I had encountered since I crossed the Mississippi River. Many of the other ladies I had traveled with had also been shown respect from others.

Of course, as in any community, there had been some who were not friendly, and a person would not want to run into them if no one else were around.

In short, the territories were nothing like what I'd expected them to be.

Chapter Six

Dawn seemed to come earlier in Montana than it had in the east. I jolted awake when my mattress moved. Blinking, I saw Simon making his way to the ladder. He must have bumped into my bed. When I turned my head to where Anna and Susan had slept, their mattress was empty. Breathing in, I smelled coffee and bacon.

So the previous day where my step-sisters had slept in had been an aberration. Feeling tired, I dragged myself out of bed and dressed in the dress I'd worn the day before. How dearly I wished I had my trunk or at least the chance to wash the clothes in my carpet bag. They would not take much more wear.

Downstairs, I found Cordelia at work in the kitchen, flipping bacon in the frying pan. There was no sign of my brother or stepsisters there or in the main living space. I knew there were cows and pigs in the barn, so I could only assume they had morning chores they were responsible for every morning.

Steeling myself for another refusal, I walked around the table and approached my stepmother. I could only continue trying. I did not want to be seen as a laggard or lazy person.

Far from it; I had worked hard at my aunt's house. Uncle Richard would not have stood for anything less.

Before I could knock on the counter or think of some other way to draw her attention, Cordelia turned toward me. Had she seen me or had she heard my footsteps? I always wondered whenever someone who hadn't been looking at me suddenly faced me. She shook her head, an expression of resignation on her face. She gestured towards the bedrooms.

"Dress...children."

Me? Dress my half-siblings? Startled by the request—or rather, the order— I blinked at her. A scowl crossed her face, and she turned her back on me. It was not an option. Not wanting to anger her anymore, I walked to the bedroom door. How hard could it be?

Both children were still fast asleep on their mattress. The all too familiar scent of urine was in the room, signaling that at least one of them had wet the bed overnight. The sheets would have to be washed. If so, perhaps I could wash my clothing at the same time. What kind of routine would Cordelia have for when she washed laundry?

Straightening my spine, I went to the small trunk that was open against the wall. Children's clothing was there, and I picked up the first appropriate outfits for them both. Then, I faced the mattress where they both slumbered. When I shook her shoulder, Katie opened her eyes, blinked, and then returned to sleep.

Grabbing her arms, I sat her up. No matter how much moving I did, she refused to open her eyes more than a slight crack. She remained malleable and half awake as I changed her out of her nightgown into the cotton dress. Her underclothes were soaked, so she was the one responsible for wetting the bed. I tossed them to the floor to take care of later.

Sam, on the other hand, opened his mouth wide as he protested being awoken from sleep. I was thankful I couldn't hear his screams, though I had no doubt Cordelia was not pleased with the situation. Nothing I did seemed to calm him, no amount of jostling. Finally, once I had his diaper changed and a fresh gown on him, I gave up all hope of calming him, and I carried him out to his mother.

She scowled and snatched him from me. Cordelia made a gesture towards the stove and then rushed back to the bedroom. Faced with the pancakes and bacon, I felt more confident with being able to handle that task.

I was kept busy making sure the bacon was fried just right, and the pancakes were the right golden color until everyone who'd gone out to care for chores came back in. While Anna carried what looked to be a bucket of milk, Susan held a small basket. She shoved it into my hands, and I looked down to see that it was filled with fresh eggs.

Before I could ask what I was expected to do with them, Cordelia came back into the kitchen, passed the still-crying Sam to Anna, and pulled the fork from my hand. She took over the meal. I could only guess that I had done well enough since she didn't glare at me or offer any disapproval.

Less than ten minutes later, Susan had the table set, and everyone was seated. Father was dressed in the suit he'd been wearing when I met him at the store. "Are you sure I can't come too?" Anna asked once prayer was said over the meal. I would have missed her question if I hadn't been reaching to take the plate of bacon from Simon, who was next to her.

"You...needed here," Father said in answer. "Simon will be all the help I need."

As at school, the more I watched them each talk, the easier it was to read their lips. While I still needed to focus on each speaker, I did not need as much concentration as before.

"What about Ivy?" Cordelia asked just before I dropped my gaze to my food.

"Ivy will help you."

From the way Cordelia's jaw tightened, that was not the answer she wanted. Did she think that because I was deaf, I was useless? Had she ignored everything I had done the day before?

"Prater will...." The rest of Father's sentence was lost to me as he looked down at his plate.

Mr. Prater would be here? That was incredibly kind of him. Did he work for my father? Was he a real cowboy?

As soon as breakfast was finished, Father and Simon set off on horseback. Cordelia went out onto the porch to watch them leave, while Anna and Susan cleared the dishes from the table. Katie sat on the floor with her doll.

When Cordelia returned, she had an air of determination about her. She set Sam on the floor with Katie and then went into the kitchen. With a gesture, she sent Susan outside and then plunged her hands into the soapy water.

Within minutes, Susan hauled in a bucket of fresh water. She seemed to be having trouble with the task, so I moved to help her. A glare from the thirteen-year-old stopped me in my tracks, though. If she would rather struggle along by herself, who was I to interfere?

My step-mother faced me. "Why are you standing there?" she demanded. "Get the laundry."

Nothing was more frustrating than being in trouble for something I did not know. Still, since I needed clothes washed, I went to the ladder. Once I was up there, I gathered everything I thought would benefit from a wash, including most of the items in my carpet bag.

Speaking of my belongings, where had my trunk been put? I hadn't seen it downstairs. Was it out in the barn? It was the only place it could be unless it had been left on the porch, though I didn't know why it hadn't been brought in like the other trunks.

Cordelia was heating up water in several large pots on the stove. She had the front door, and all the windows open allow the breeze to freshen the house. Without even looking at me, she waved for me to carry my load outside.

Anna had already dragged a washtub into place and put the washboard inside. When she saw me with my arms full of dirty clothes, she rolled her eyes and shook her head with open disgust. She darted into the house and returned with two large baskets. As I watched, she tossed one at my feet and carefully set the second by the washtub.

If I had seen them inside, I would have used one, but I hadn't. I didn't know where she had found them. Anna turned away before I could ask her. No doubt she would have ignored me even if I had asked.

I dropped the dirty laundry into the basket and watched as my step-sister stretched a narrow rope between two trees. The line sagged in the middle and before I could offer to help her, Mr. Prater appeared on the opposite end, pulling the string taut. Anna's face immediately brightened, and she tossed her braid over her shoulder.

As soon as the line was tied into place, she rushed over to speak to him. Whatever she said was met with him tipping his hat, and he turned away. My gaze caught his, and he nodded in my direction. He went toward the barn, though to do what, I didn't know.

Cordelia brought out the first of the pans of water and dumped it into the washtub. Anna returned to the tub and picked up the basket of laundry. Without a care to the fabrics or colors, she dropped them all in. I couldn't keep from cringing. I'd always separated each item, leaving the delicates for last as they needed more care.

Noticing my expression, Anna sent a challenging look at me and tossed a bar of soap in my direction. As I managed to catch it, she walked away. I was never one to back down from a challenge so, rolling up my sleeves, I stepped forward. I'd done the wash in Springfield often enough.

How difficult would it be to do it for just a few more people?

The second tub was filled with water as I began to scrub the first of many clothes. Within minutes, my fingers were wrinkled and raw from the soap and hot water. For the difficult stains, I had the bar of soap to use on them. My arms began to ache from the work.

As soon as I was done with one garment, I would wring it out and toss it into the second tub. Anna would then rinse the soap free and fill a basket with the clean clothes. She carried the wet clothes to the line and hung them up, pinning them in place with clothespins.

Hours went by with this work. Though she kept inside, now and then, Cordelia would come out and inspect our work. Each time, she'd find something not entirely up to her standards and the garment would be thrown back into my tub. She wouldn't say what was wrong, sometimes I couldn't even see it, but I would obediently rewash it.

What else could I have done?

Once in awhile, I would see Mr. Prater go in and out of the barn, involved in whatever work he was doing. Every time, Anna would pause and smooth her dress or hair. She gave every indication that she was smitten with the young man, and I couldn't blame her. He was handsome and, as far as I could tell, kind. Only a fool would be disinterested in a man like that.

Still, a twinge of jealousy twisted inside of me every time. Anna was pretty, and though she hadn't been kind to me, maybe she wasn't like that with other people, so it was possible Mr. Prater liked her in return.

So I focused on my work, working out stains from the cloth. By the end of the day, it was all dry and folded, put back in the right places. I was proud of what had been accomplished. Why wouldn't I be?

Any statement of "well done," or "good job," or anything like that from my stepmother would have been too much to expect, but I thought I'd get something from my father. Instead, as soon as he entered he had words of praise for Cordelia's work in arranging the house. He lifted up Sam and Katie and tugged on Susan's braid.

All he had for me was a brief smile, and then he was talking to Cordelia, his back to me. Simon went straight to the ladder and vanished upstairs. I tried to hide my disappointment by focusing on the mending in my hand. By washing clothes, I had discovered many holes and rips that were in need of fixing. Cordelia had been busy putting things how she wanted, and her daughters had helped her, so the task had fallen to me.

It was a good thing I enjoyed sewing. I knew some girls found it tedious, but I loved the creative outlet it gave me almost as much as I adored drawing. My paper and charcoal were at the bottom of my trunk, which I still hadn't located.

Supper was simple, much the same as our Sunday noon meal had been. This time, after everyone was done eating, Anna said something to her mother, deliberately hiding her face. When Cordelia gestured for me to clear the table, I knew what they had talked about.

Not that I minded. I wanted to help! The way they went about it, turning away or holding their hands over their mouths, so I wouldn't see what they said was aggravating. Maybe if I had heard and they whispered, I would have felt the same way.

I had Susan to help dry the dishes. It was only when I turned when the task was done that I saw Anna sitting by the fire, reading. Telling myself that Anna had done the dishes the previous two nights did little to rein in my outrage.

Time, I told myself. It would take time for us all to adjust. Although, maybe I wouldn't be there long enough for there to be a need for a routine.

Chapter Seven

Tuesday dawned cloudy with darker clouds on the horizon. Anna rode into town with Simon and Father to help with the store. That left me to help Cordelia with the ironing.

Most of the time, she was distracted by the small children. Susan spent the day outside, weeding the small garden. My trunk was still missing, and every moment I thought I'd be able to go in search of it, Cordelia demanded me to get back to work. Every time I asked after it, twice in writing and once vocally, I was ignored.

Besides the change in task, the day passed more or less as the previous had, ending precisely the same: my work ignored while Father praised Cordelia's and Susan's.

Wednesday, as it turned out, was the day for mending, which I had begun on Monday. Simon remained behind to put together the bed frames for everyone in the attic, and then he joined Mr. Prater—I still had yet to learn his first name—to do repairs to fences and the roof of the barn.

Though I offered, through gestures, to take lunch out to them, Cordelia sent Susan, who was more than happy to abandon her needlework.

Selfishly, I was delighted when a quick comparison revealed that my stitches were smaller and more even than my stepmother's. It felt good to have something I was good at, whether anyone else noticed or not. But it would have been nice for my work to have been recognized.

Thursday's task was to put away everything that had been washed, mended, and ironed the previous days. To have these tasks spread out over three days confused me. They all were difficult, it was true, but was it so hard to put things away immediately?

I tried to ask my stepmother, but her expression of disgust when she read the question made me think this was how it was always done.

On Friday, while Cordelia and Anna became dusted with flour from baking, I was tasked with doing a small load of washing. The baby went through many diapers each day, and little Katie had not yet stopped wetting the bed. After several days, the smell was intolerable.

The task went quickly, and while the cloth waved in the breeze, I took advantage of the time to enter the barn. Mr. Prater looked up from where he was repairing a harness and stood up. It was the first time his hat was nowhere to be seen.

"Can I help you?" he asked. His expression was so serious. Did he ever smile?

Did he smile for Anna?

Shoving that jealous thought to the back of my mind where it belonged, I gestured with my hands, miming a box in the air. If I'd known he or anyone else would be in there, I would have gotten my slate. I tried to keep it on hand, but there were sometimes, like when I was up to my elbows in soapy water, when it was inconvenient.

"—need...box?" he asked with a frown.

Close, but not quite right. I shook my head and knelt down. I held my hand about how tall I thought my trunk was and then held my hand apart with the width. I looked up at him and mouthed, "Trunk."

Understanding dawned, and he gave a nod. Relieved, I stood up and then followed him further into the barn. In one of the unused horse stalls was my trunk. Delighted, I automatically signed, "Thank you!" as I rushed to it.

I didn't pause for a moment as I knelt down to open it. The scent of the lavender I had packed to keep my clothes fresh drifted up as soon as the lid opened. It put me in mind of my aunt when I breathed it in.

Knowing there wouldn't be enough room for me to take my trunk in, I rifled through my belongings. I selected two dresses, one being my Sunday best, and also I pulled out my sketchbook. The rest could wait.

After all, what would be the point of unpacking it all if I was only going to ask Father about returning to Hartford?

Pleased with myself, I sent a smile at Mr. Prater and carried a small armload of my clothes out of the barn. My stepmother stood by the washtub, her hands on her hips. It wasn't until I followed her gaze that I understood why she appeared to be angry.

All the white diapers I had pinned to the clothesline were on the ground.

Dumbfounded, I stared at them. How had they managed to come loose? I'd been careful to secure them to the line, and there was hardly a breeze to have pulled them down.

Cordelia faced me, and her eyes went to the clothes I held. She strode towards me and reached out as though she wanted to rip them out of my arms. Instinctively, I turned away, tightening my grip. At the same time, the word "Mine!" left my lips.

Out of the corner of my eye, I saw Cordelia's hand come up, and I flinched back a step, bracing myself for the blow I expected to land. When it didn't come, and Cordelia's hand went to her head as though she were smoothing her black hair down, I straightened and turned to see what had convinced her to stay her hand.

Mr. Prater was leading one of the horses out. Had he glanced over, and my stepmother thought better of striking me? I had to believe it was so as I turned my gaze back to the woman.

"Go inside," she said, the muscles of her jaw twitching. "I'll clean up your mess."

With that said, Cordelia started for the line. She believed I was at fault? How could she?

Ducking my head, I made a beeline for the house. For a moment, Anna blocked my way, a scowl marring her face. I stepped up to her so that we were inches apart. Just when I thought she would shove me off the step, she moved aside, and I was able to hurry in.

The sooner I spoke to Father about returning East, the better it would be for us all.

FRIDAY EVENING I HAD no chance to talk to my father. Saturday morning he left early to get to the store as soon as he could. Once again, I was left to do whatever tasks Cordelia could devise for me.

She sent me out to work in the garden, putting Susan in charge of me. The thirteen-year-old stood over me and smacked my hand every time I reached for a valuable plant.

I'd never pulled weeds before. Any vegetables Aunt Ruth needed, she would purchase, so I knew how to bargain with those who sold vegetables. Growing them was an entirely different matter.

By the time I reached the end of a row, I was hot, dripping with sweat, and dirty. I leaned back on my heels as I took a break. Susan had abandoned her job of watching over me, and I had no idea where she had gone.

As I glanced around, I saw Mr. Prater over by the empty corral. My gaze caught his and then he made a sharp jerk with his head towards the barn. When I moved my gaze to the structure, though, I didn't see anything. The young man had already returned his focus to his work when I glanced at him again.

My curiosity piqued, I stood up and walked over. The barn door was open, and I saw movement inside: the edge of a brown calico dress going into the stall where my trunk was located. Appalled, I rushed in.

Cordelia and Anna were standing over my trunk, which was open. In my stepsister's hands was my best dress and my stepmother was holding my other two. A cry must have left my lips because they both spun around with startled expressions. For an instant, shame was written on their faces.

They knew what they were doing was wrong. Those were my dresses, in my trunk.

"What are you doing?" Cordelia asked, her shame shifting to anger. "...can...be finished."

There was no way I was going to let her turn the situation on me. I strode forward and grabbed the skirt of one of the dresses she held. At the same time, I brought my free hand to my chest. Mine!

Where she had backed down the day before, Cordelia refused to let go of the dresses. What use would they be to her? I was much smaller than both she and her daughter, so my dresses would not fit them. Was it merely that they didn't want me to have them?

"Finish you...chore," Cordelia said.

"No!" The word was easy to say, and I slashed through the air with my hand. I wasn't going anywhere until I was sure every one of my belongings was where it should be. For emphasis, I tugged on the dress.

Her grip didn't loosen at all. "I will tell your father."

As if I thought that a threat! I was in the right! Abruptly, Anna dropped the dress she held and stepped forward. Her expression was cheerful. "We...helping her..." she said.

Cordelia turned, and a flash of annoyance appeared on her face. "Will."

Twisting around, all the while keeping the fabric fisted in my hand, I saw Mr. Prater had entered the barn. He swapped out hammers, not showing a bit of interest in what was happening. With a tip of his hat, he walked back out.

Was his first name Will?

Anna said something to her mother, and Cordelia released her grip on the dresses. They left the barn, and I was quick to pick up my garments. Dust marred the fabric, but otherwise, they seemed unharmed.

Would my stepmother have damaged the dresses if I hadn't been warned that they were in my trunk? I'd faced prejudice against me due to my lack of hearing, but this was beyond ridiculous!

In any event, she would learn that I was not one to be taken advantage of! She was not the first to try, and I would hold my ground just as I had every other time. Once Father knew what she had done, he would be on my side.

Wouldn't he?

The fact that I wasn't sure broke my heart.

THOUGH CORDELIA HAD me toting buckets of water inside, I kept a close watch for my father. My note detailing everything I had endured was in my pocket. All I would have to do was get it into his hand before Cordelia had a chance to say anything.

So the moment I saw the horses enter the yard, I dropped the bucket of water and ran to meet them at the barn. Father's face was lined with weariness. He must have had a long day, and what I was about to tell him would only add to it. "Father!"

Instead of hugging me as a greeting, he took my shoulders and moved me to the side. I refused to be put off, though. "Papa." I pushed the paper into his hand, using my right hand to make a circle on my chest. Please.

He closed his eyes for a moment and then passed the reins to Simon, who was watching with undisguised interest. Father held the note up, and his eyes moved across the page. When he was done, he pinched the bridge of his nose. He looked up suddenly and said, "Cordelia."

I turned to see my stepmother coming from the house. Her expression was furious. She must have realized I would tell my father what had happened. And then she started speaking.

"Whatever she...told you, she is a liar."

How dare she call me a liar? Father raised his eyebrow and handed her my letter. I watched her as she read my words. A blush crept up her neck onto her cheeks. I'd kept the account short and had used blunt words, leaving nothing out. She finally lowered the letter.

"Do...believe her and not me?" she asked, a challenge in her eyes.

Did she just ask my father, her husband, to chose between the two of us? Horrified, I stared at her. Was she so threatened by me that she thought it was necessary?

The stress on Father's face didn't ease. Beyond Cordelia, I saw Anna on the porch. Even though she was as much a part of this, it was her mother who had instigated it.

"Dear, why did you go into Ivy's trunk?" Father asked.

"Why shouldn't I?" Cordelia asked, her eyes sparkling with sudden tears. "Why should she have more than the rest of us?"

Was that her reasoning? My clothes wouldn't have fit her or Anna! Did she expect to take my dress and cut it down for Susan, who was close to my height already, or for Katie?

There was nothing else in my trunk that would be useful to anyone, beyond the books which I was more than happy to share. My paper was for sketching, and my underclothes were fitted to me.

"Why...you ask why she... rude? Refuses to do as I say?"

Father turned slightly so that I couldn't read his lips anymore. Whatever he said made Cordelia more agitated. She stepped closer, and I moved aside so that I wasn't between them.

Simon shook his head and led the horses to the barn. Whatever was being said was no doubt uncomfortable to overhear. For once, I was glad I couldn't hear it, and though I felt a little guilty for being the reason for the discussion, I was proud I'd stood up for myself.

After much head shaking, Father faced me. His expression was a mixture of disappointment and resignation. "Let's go inside."

It was ridiculous to stand in the middle of the yard for this argument. Cordelia spun on her heel and marched to the house. She swatted at Katie, who was unfortunate enough to have gotten in her mother's path.

Inside, the smell of roasting chicken filled the air. It would have made my mouth water if I weren't so angry. Father handed me the now crumpled paper I'd written my explanation on and gestured to his desk. Confused, I frowned. What did he expect me to write? Hadn't my first note been clear enough?

"Ivy...you disobey your mother?"

The question made my hands come up. "She is not my mother. And the only time I 'disobeyed' was when I had to protect what belongs to me!" I signed all of this at lightning speed as I tended to do whenever I became upset. "If you don't want me here, send me back to Hartford!"

Naturally, Father could not have understood me, but how else did he expect me to answer his question? With a frown, he pointed at the desk.

If he wanted me to write the words, I was more than happy to oblige. My pen strokes were harsher than necessary, slashing across the paper with undisguised fury. Once I finished my explanation of why I had refused to do as Cordelia had asked and my request to be sent back to school, I handed it over with a feeling of victory.

Father read it, his expression remaining neutral. He shook his head once again and looked straight at me. "I...disappointed in you, Ivy," he said.

Disappointed? In me?

"Anna, watch the water!" Cordelia said at that moment. She looked pleased which did not bode well for me. "Set the table!"

With Sam on her hip, Anna hurried into the kitchen. There were multiple large pots on the stovetop, steam rising from them all. Did I dare hope there would be a bath in my future? I couldn't think about that and focused on Father.

His gaze was on his wife. "I'm...Ivy won't cause more trouble," he said. He glanced at me. "I...make her understand she... contributes."

I was the victim, and yet I was to be the one in trouble? None of the times I had faced injustice hurt as much as it did at that moment. My hand trembling, I reached over and pointed to my request to return to school.

My heart dropped as Father shook his head. He crumbled the paper in his hand and turned away.

I wasn't going back.

IT WOULD HAVE BEEN dramatic to take myself to my bed and refuse supper, but I was above that. I did, however, refuse to make eye contact with anyone. The satisfaction on Cordelia's face was more than I could stomach.

Without waiting to be ordered to do it, I cleared the table and began to wash the dishes. Anna carried hot water out and helped her mother bathe Sam and Katie. Susan dried the dishes, and we both put them away.

Next in the bathtub was Cordelia. She sat in front of the fireplace and combed her hair out. Susan vanished for fifteen minutes, and when she returned, Anna was quick to go out.

Anna was longer, so I was ready when she came in. The sky was darkening when I stepped into the cloudy, quickly cooling water. As far as baths go, it was not relaxing, but it was a relief to wash the dirt and sweat from my skin.

Simon brushed past me with a scowl when I walked into the room. Cordelia was combing out Katie's hair, and Father was bent over an accounts book at the table. I had little desire to be near any of them and retreated to my attic bed to comb my hair by the light of a small candle.

Morning brought me no calm spirit. In the hope that being in church would achieve this, I dressed in the mauve dress I'd pulled from my trunk. I'd embroidered black ivy along the hem and on the sleeves to add a touch of fanciness.

When I climbed down the ladder, I couldn't help but see Cordelia glare in my direction. She turned her back on whatever was cooking in the frying pan to face me directly. Her movement seemed almost mocking.

"Milk. The. Cow."

She made a point to enunciate each word, and it made me mad. I shook my head, using one finger to tap my temple as I did so. I don't know how. My stepmother's glare intensified. "Don't make me tell your father."

Her gaze moved beyond me, and I spun around to see Father coming out of the bedroom. Tiredness hung on him still. "Ivy, do as she says."

Raising my chin, I walked to the desk and pulled a sheet of paper out. *I don't know how to milk a cow*, I wrote. Turning around, I carried my note to Father and handed it to him. Why would he think I would know how to do this? In Springfield, milk was delivered to our doorstep every morning.

As he read my one sentence, Father rubbed the side of his head, and he walked out of the house. It seemed at every turn I disappointed him. The feeling was mutual because he continued to disappoint me.

Smelling bacon about to burn, I glanced over at the stove. Cordelia was coming toward me, fury on her face. "Worthless girl!" she said, raising her hand. "Do...think we will bow to your every whim?"

Her hand swung towards me, and I grabbed her wrist. She gave a start, apparently not having expected me to stop her. Little did she know Uncle Richard had honed my reflexes, though it had always been a risk to evade his blows.

If Aunt Ruth hadn't been nearby to intervene, it would only make him angrier.

For a moment, Cordelia and I stared at each other. She jerked out of my grasp and returned to the kitchen. No doubt she would blame me for the burnt bacon, which was a stretch since she didn't like me in her kitchen.

One by one, my step-sisters came down, followed by Simon. It seemed strange that I was the early riser among them when they'd grown up in this life, and my brother had had ten years to adjust to it. A word from Cordelia sent them scattering to their chores. Anna and Simon rushed outside, and Susan ran to the toddlers.

I went to the kitchen and set the table. Cordelia's back was tense every time I went past her. If Father had been serious and I wasn't leaving the Montana territory, then she and I would have to find some way of living together in the same house.

What kind of future would I have in Montana? Father had left me in the East for a reason. It was true I was older and able to take care of myself more, but was it enough to survive? These thoughts went round and round in my mind throughout the simple breakfast. I kept my eyes downward, so I didn't see if anyone commented about the burnt bacon that was served up with the scrambled eggs.

Dishes had to be washed and put away quickly. All too soon most of us were in the wagon and headed to town. I remained near the back while Anna tried to keep Katie from climbing over the wagon seat to be with Father and Cordelia. Simon rode his horse behind, looking bored with the entire excursion.

The sky was cloudy, which meant it was slightly cooler, so I didn't become sweaty from the sun beating down on me. We arrived at the church just as everyone was filing in. As soon as Father set the brake of the wagon and climbed down, Cordelia handed Sam to him and climbed down. Sending what I assumed were commands for us all to hurry up, she rushed for the door.

Anna passed Katie to Simon before she climbed out and Susan jumped down without any help. I was the last one to reach the ground, and when I followed my family in, I ended up with the aisle seat of the pew.

The rest of the congregation had stood for a hymn, so we weren't too conspicuous. Like the week before, because we were in the back and Simon didn't bother to share the hymn book with me, I didn't understand any of what was going on, and my attention wandered. My focus went straight to the squirrel head I could see peeking out of a boy's pocket three pews up and to the left.

I lost sight of it when everyone sat, and the reverend began his sermon. How had the boy caught the squirrel and why was he keeping it in his pocket?

Before too long, the squirrel made a reappearance. It landed on the floor next to the pew and made a break for freedom. I couldn't tear my eyes away from it as it bolted down the aisle. Something behind me startled it, though, and it made a split second decision. It vanished right under my skirts.

Chapter Eight

The skirts of my dress were full to accommodate the hoops I'd packed separately and was still waiting to arrive. I didn't immediately feel the creature, but I knew he was there.

Simon's elbow jabbed me in the side. I must have made some sound of surprise. No one else seemed to have noticed the rogue rodent. Its tail brushed against my legs, and I bit my lip to hold in my amusement. My brother jabbed me again, so I must not have been successful in that endeavor.

The people in the opposite pew looked over and in front of me, the gentleman twisted around to see what was happening, though his wife hissed something at him that made him face the reverend again. I didn't have to look to know I had drawn my family's attention as well.

It was hard to ignore the squirrel climbing my petticoats, and there was no way for me to explain. I couldn't whisper and speaking up in the middle of the sermon would have been rude. Steadfastly, I stared at the reverend, hoping the critter would abandon its hiding place sooner rather than later. My cheeks burned, but I managed to make it through the rest of the service.

I don't know what it was doing under my skirt, but it kept moving and climbing. While I was sure its tiny claws were doing damage to the fabric, I couldn't blame it for wanting some peace and safety and if I lost a petticoat in the process, so be it.

Finally, as everyone stood up for the last hymn, though I decided to remain unmoving for obvious reasons, the poor squirrel decided to make his escape. As it happened, he chose the route that took him right over the shoes of my family. I couldn't hold back laughter as panic spread through the pew.

There was nothing like seeing a grown woman scramble onto a pew. Perhaps it was cruel of me to be so amused by Cordelia's actions, which Anna imitated on the other end of the bench. Their open mouths told me they were screaming as well. I lost sight of the poor squirrel and could only hope he found some way to freedom.

I was pleased to see that I wasn't the only one laughing. My family had attracted the attention of everyone in the room. Father had his hand over his face, and Simon's shoulders shook with laughter.

After several minutes, when red-faced Cordelia stepped from the pew, and it seemed as though the panic was over, the congregation carried on with the last hymn.

If they'd ever had a more exciting Sunday, I wanted someone to tell me what it was, because a squirrel running loose in the church had to be hard to beat.

CORDELIA AND FATHER were quick to herd us all out as soon as the prayer was done. I suppose neither of them wanted to face the amusement of their friends and neighbors. They weren't fast enough though, for a tall young man in a suit approached us at the wagon. He took off his hat, revealing slicked back black hair.

"Hello Mr. Steele," he said. His face was not as tanned as most men I'd seen, so he must not work outside. The suit he wore also looked to be of a finer quality than my father's. It was his pale gray eyes that unsettled me. "I'm glad I caught up to—"

Sending a quick look at Cordelia, Father shook the man's hand. Since I was behind my father, I couldn't read his lips to know what he was saying. The young man kept looking at me as he nodded, agreeing with whatever Father said to him. He seemed to be friendly, however, I knew better than to trust outward appearances.

I'd met many people since I became deaf, and most of the time I had a gut feeling from the start about who I could trust and who it would be better to avoid. The young man by the wagon made my skin crawl the way he looked at me, and I put him in the "avoid" category.

"Might I meet your daughter?" he asked after several minutes of conversation with Father.

Me? He wanted to meet me? Why? Father must not have thought anything of it because he gestured to me. The young man nodded towards me with a broad smile. "Pleasure to meet you, Miss Steele."

Well, he knew my name, but I didn't know his. Still, I nodded acknowledgment and moved my gaze to the back of the wagon seat. A moment later, Father was in the seat, and the wagon was rolling.

My curiosity got the better of me. I tapped Anna's shoulder and signed, "Who was that?" I made sure to mouth "who" at the same time she would understand me. Instead of answering me, though, she just glared.

It wasn't much of a stretch that she was angry with me. I turned to Simon and, once I waved to him and got his attention, I asked the same question of him. He glanced at Father before he said, "John Dover."

At least I now had a name to put with the face.

Though neither of them looked at me, I had the feeling Father and Cordelia were discussing what had happened. "Discuss" was probably not the most accurate term for it. They kept looking at each other, their shoulders tense. I couldn't see what either of them were saying, and no doubt it was better that way.

What had the family been like before I arrived? They must have been happy and gotten along. What was it about me that had disrupted things so much? Was it only because I was deaf, different from them? Or was there something more?

I knew I shouldn't feel guilty. After all, it wasn't my fault I was deaf. There wasn't anyone to blame for that; it had been beyond anyone's control. And Father should have told his wife about me, not making it so that my arrival would upset her so.

Still, I did feel guilty.

It seemed I had brought nothing but trouble into Father's life. Every day he had some argument with Cordelia. My stepmother had no affection for me. My brother and step-siblings would rather ignore me than anything else.

Everything Uncle Richard had said about me had come true. I closed my eyes, pushing away the memory of his harsh words. My thoughts were troubled the entire drive back to the ranch.

Cordelia swept into the house without a glance back as soon as Father halted the wagon in front of the porch. Anna ceased glaring at me to hurry after her mother. Father leaned his head back and stared at the sky. Simon dismounted and helped Susan and Katie down to the ground. He sent a wink at me when I climbed down.

Maybe be Father, and Cordelia's argument hadn't been serious? It seemed too good to be true.

As Father and Simon went to the barn, I took a deep breath and went onto the porch. For a moment, I stood in the doorway and watched my stepmother slam things around the kitchen. Anna had Katie and Sam in front of the fireplace.

Apparently, it was better for me to keep my distance until Cordelia calmed down.

SITTING ON THE EDGE of my bed, I spent the day writing the letters I should have written as soon as I had arrived. I had been so busy it hadn't even occurred to me to let Mrs. Weston, the reverand's wife back East, know I'd arrived safely. She must be worried about me, and of course, my friends from school would be curious about where I was.

Occasionally, Simon would pass by, and he looked as though he was interested in what I was doing, but he never asked. Anna tried to peek at my words, but she moved away when I stared at her. I don't know why I was surprised since she had gone through my trunk. She must have no sense of right or wrong. My letters were private, and she had no business trying to look at what I was saying.

Imagine what it would have been like if I'd had a journal!

That evening, Mr. Prater joined us for dinner and from what I gathered, he'd moved into the back of the barn. I think if he hadn't been there, supper would have been another awkward, tense meal. As it was, Anna kept up lively dialogue, mostly directed at our guest. As usual, no one had anything to say to me.

I was ignored by my step-sisters when we changed into our nightgowns. They finished before me, and since I hadn't thought ahead to keep the candle close, they blew it out before I was ready.

What would it take for them not to be antagonistic towards me?

Morning dawned with no answers for me. I slipped my letters into my pocket when I went downstairs. Without saying a word, Cordelia handed me the basket I recognized as the one used for eggs.

Well, it looked like it was time to learn something new.

The chickens, especially those sitting on their nests, were not impressed with me invading their coop. The creatures pecked at my hands when I reached into the straw. By the time I had located the eggs, my right hand was bleeding. How did Susan and Anna do this every day and not have scarred hands?

As I was carrying the eggs away from the coop, I encountered Mr. Prater. He took one look at my hand and shook his head. He motioned for me to follow him and he went to the back of the chicken coop where there was a wooden container. Inside was corn. Mr. Prater took a handful and tossed it at the chickens.

To my amazement, all the chickens flew out of the coop and began pecking at the ground. So, that's how to get them out of their nests. Why hadn't anyone told me this? Everyone assumed I knew how to do these kinds of things. I should have swallowed my pride and asked for instruction, but the way my step-sisters behaved around me....they wouldn't have told me.

After I signed 'thank you' to Mr. Prater, I quickly carried in the eggs. Cordelia saw the blood on my hand, but her expression didn't change. Once I gave her the eggs, I went out to wash the blood from my skin.

Mr. Prater joined us for breakfast. Since he'd moved onto the ranch, it seemed he would have all of his meals with us.

When Father put on his hat to go into town, I held out my correspondence to him. There was no mistaking the shock on his face as he took the five sealed letters from me. "Who are these for?" he asked.

"My friends," I signed, linking my index fingers together. I made sure I mouthed the words at the same time. While I wanted my family to understand me, I wasn't willing to abandon sign language even if it did frustrate them.

Father seemed to understand because he nodded. His expression, though, was one of shame. Had he assumed I didn't have any friends? Did he think a deaf person didn't make connections with other people?

Without another word, Father left, putting my letters in his pocket as he went through the doorway. I stepped out on the porch to watch him, and Simon set off on horseback. I wanted to see what else the Montana territory had to hold, but it looked like I was going to remain on the ranch.

Another week began, and the same routine Cordelia had followed previously came into play. Monday was the day for laundry. The day was sunny, so everything dried quickly on the clothesline. Once again, there were damp sheets from Katie's inability to go an entire night without wetting the bed.

On Tuesday, we ironed everything we'd washed the day before. I burned my finger on the hot iron when I tested the temperature. Wednesday was the day for mending, and Cordelia scowled when she noticed how small my stitches were. Anything I did well, she became angry about.

Thursday was spent putting the washed, ironed and mended clothing away, and the upstairs was cleaned. Anna and I hung all the quilts out to air out on the clothesline. When Friday dawned, I again washed diapers while Cordelia baked.

Part of me was glad to have a routine, but the other half of me was irritated by the number of chores Cordelia ordered done. Every time I tried to ask Father about why I could not return to school, she would have something for me to do and Father would tell me to do as I was told.

Susan no longer supervised me when we weeded the garden. Instead, she was down on her knees helping me. She, at least, had decided not to be angry with me. Or maybe it was just that she was ignoring me like everyone else and wasn't being antagonistic about it.

By the time Sunday arrived, I was ready to see something other than the yard around the house. Breakfast was served, and everyone seemed to take their time eating. All at once, though, everyone was rising from the table. Instead of clearing the dishes to wash, Anna grabbed her shawl from the hook by the door. She ushered Katie and Susan out the door with Simon close behind. Cordelia slung her shawl over her shoulders and picked up Sam while Father put his hat on.

Why were they leaving the dishes on the table?

Cordelia glanced at me and then turned her head to Father, so I couldn't see whatever she said. I took a step towards them, ready for the drive into town, but Father held up his hand. Confused, I came to a stop.

"Ivy, it would be best for you to stay here."

What? He couldn't mean that. "Why?" I was so surprised I didn't even sign the word.

Father glanced at his wife, but she was fussing with the blanket she had wrapped around Sam. "Cordelia and I agree it will be easier for you."

So I would be left with the dishes, left alone on the ranch, while they went to town. As I struggled to think of an argument so I could go, they walked out of the house.

Chapter Nine

I tried to maintain calm as I watched my family ride away from the house in the wagon, leaving me standing on the porch. Tears blurred my vision, though I managed to keep my chin up. No matter what, I couldn't let them see how they'd hurt me. As soon as I was certain they would not see, I bolted away from the house.

My hand pressed against my mouth, I stumbled my way through the long grass. When I felt as though it would be too much to go another step forward, I fell onto my knees. Angry, frustrated, and full of grief, I screamed at the sky. Even though I couldn't hear my pain, it felt good to release it.

Was this what my life would be like from now on? Kept on the ranch, far from anyone else, as though I were someone shameful? Why would Father allow this to happen? Was he, too, ashamed of me?

Tears ran down my cheeks, unhindered. More than ever, I missed Hartford and the school. It had done wonders for my confidence to learn and be among those who understood me. Not that I meant to put the school on a pedestal, but it was hard not to.

I'd already endured the stifling judgment of Uncle Richard and now to be confronted with the humiliation of being a pariah in my own family was more than I could stand.

Sitting back, I drew my knees to my chest and wrapped my arms around them. I rested my cheek on my knees and closed my eyes. There was a place I dreamed of, a town I had visited one summer. My good friend, Nina, came from there and had wanted to share her world with me. She came from Chilmark, a town where a majority of people were born deaf and those who weren't still understood sign.

It had been like paradise. There had been a noticeable difference between the signing there and what I had learned in school. Still, to walk down the street and see others freely signing, carrying on a conversation without being stared at by passersby, had been eye-opening.

To expect such in Montana would have naïve, but why not something similar in my own family? It wouldn't be that difficult to learn a few signs, but no one had even attempted to understand me. They just expected me to conform to the ways they knew how to communicate: through writing and miming.

I'm not sure why that bothered me as much as it did. After all, I'd communicated with Aunt Ruth with writing and most anyone else I came across, but it was...tiring. Was this how immigrants, just stepping onto America's shores, felt? Having their own culture, language, traditions, and being expected to conform?

In any event, I'd never felt so alone, not even when I first became deaf.

The sun warmed my back as I sat in the grass. I don't know how long I sat there, feeling sorry for myself. Sniffing, I finally lifted my head and opened my eyes. Immediately, I gave a start. Mr. Prater was sitting a few yards away from me, staring off at the horizon. His hat was tipped back so that the sun would hit his face.

Ashamed he'd caught me sulking, I mopped at my face with the sleeve of my dress, wishing I'd put a handkerchief in my pocket or had an apron to use instead. When I looked up again, he'd turned his head and raised his eyebrow. A blush heated up my cheeks, but I didn't drop my gaze.

"Are you ...ell?" he asked.

Was I Elle? He knew my name was Ivy so that not must have been what he said. Had he asked if I was ill? That was close to what I thought he'd said. Or had he asked if I was well? He seemed to see my hesitation, and he asked, "Are you all right?"

My curiosity piqued as to why he was here and not at church like everyone else, I gave a brief nod. With an answering nod, he pushed himself off the ground. I expected him to leave and get back to whatever it was he had been in the middle of before he thought to check on me. Instead, he came over and offered his hand to me. Cautiously, I put my hand in his, and he pulled me to my feet. As times before, I breathed in the scent of pine and horse.

"...not safe to wander..." He released my hand and stepped back.

I nodded again, glancing over my shoulder. I hadn't realized I had run quite so far in my desire to escape the house. It was barely visible in the distance. Before I even realized I was doing it, I brought my hand up to my chest and made a circle. Sorry.

A slight frown formed on his face, and he tilted his head. My blush intensified, and I dropped my hand. I'd rushed off without my slate, and I mentally kicked myself for having done so. To my amazement, though, he mimicked the gesture I had made, making a circle with his hand over his chest.

"What does that mean?"

He wanted to know, really know, what the sign meant? I mouthed the word, *'Sorry'* hoping that it would be enough. A look of confusion was still on his face, though, so I repeated it. This time, he nodded in understanding.

"What do...have to be sorry for?"

It would have been too hard to explain, so I lifted my shoulders in a shrug. He rubbed the back of his neck, sending a glance around. After a moment, he seemed to come to a decision, and he held his hand out to me.

"Come with me."

For a moment, I just stared at his hand. Where did he want to take me? He was the one person to be kind to me since I had arrived in the territory. Granted, I had only met him and my family, so I would hope there were other thoughtful people. I just hadn't met them yet. However, that wasn't important right then.

Having no reason not to trust him, I put my hand in his. The corners of his mouth quirked as though he were fighting a smile. There had only been a few times I'd seen him smile. Most of the time, he looked serious, almost as though he had the weight of the world on his shoulders.

In any event, he turned and led me through the grass in the direction of the house. I couldn't think of the ranch house as home. Maybe a week was too soon to expect it to feel like home. Or was it that a place could not be home and a prison at the same time?

We reached the yard within ten minutes. I hadn't gotten as far as I thought, which was a sobering thought. Mr. Prater—Will didn't seem to fit him, and I wasn't completely sure it was his first name—angled so that we walked toward the barn and not the house as I had expected.

The barn doors stood open, and he led me inside. As I walked, I breathed in the scent of hay and wood. For a moment, I wondered why he had brought me here. To show me my trunk had been invaded again? But instead of going to the unused stall where my trunk was kept, he paused at the first stall. He let go of my hand and opened the door.

In a second I realized why he was still on the ranch and not in town with everyone else. A small brown horse was lying on the ground, its chest heaving. From the swollen belly, I guessed it was pregnant and about to give birth. Of course, someone would need to remain with it, and I wasn't sure my father had that kind of knowledge.

Stepping into the stall, Mr. Prater knelt down and ran his hand along the poor animal's neck. His presence seemed to calm her. Glancing over, he gestured for me to join him. Immediately, I shook my head. I had little experience with horses and had only been close to them when necessity had demanded it.

The young man raised his eyebrow, his expression a mixture of amusement and disbelief. There was the hint of a challenge in his dark eyes. Heaving a sigh, I stepped into the stall and took slow steps towards the animal. As soon as I did, the horse tossed its head and struggled to move. I froze, and Mr. Prater was quick to pat the horse, calming it.

After a moment, he waved for me to keep coming. Letting out the breath I hadn't realized I was holding, I tiptoed through the manure and knelt down beside him. He took my hand and brought it to the horse's neck. I was amazed to feel the hair, which was stiffer than I'd expected and not soft. I felt the beat of the horse's heart. The unfortunate thing was essentially helpless in her condition, and my heart went out to her.

Mr. Prater lifted his hand, but I left mine on the horse's neck. When I looked over, the young man was watching me. He moved his gaze to the horse and then back to me. When I didn't move, he did it again. He said, enunciating, if the slowness was anything to go by, "Horse?"

Oh, was he asking how I would sign "horse"? I lifted my hand to my head and with two fingers, made the sign. He repeated the sign perfectly, and I nodded. Of all the people I'd expected to teach my language to, this young man had never crossed my mind.

He turned his attention back to the horse. It was then I remembered the dishes that were still on the table. Reluctant to leave the peaceful atmosphere, I nonetheless stood up. Mr. Prater sent a quizzical glance at me.

"Thank you," I signed and mouthed at the same time. He gave a nod, and I retreated from the stall.

When I stepped out into the sunlight, I felt a thousand times better than I had a half hour ago. Maybe I wasn't as alone as I thought. Maybe staying in Montana wasn't so bad.

SINCE THERE WAS NO need for me to be in my good frock, I changed into my everyday dress before I set myself to my task. The breakfast dishes didn't take long to wash, dry, and put away. With nothing else to do, I carried my sketch paper and charcoal sticks out to the porch with my copy of Hamlet.

I could have put something together for the midday meal, but Cordelia objected to me using anything in her kitchen. Also, I had no idea when they would return, and if anything I made became cold or tough, I was certain I would be in trouble for it.

In short, I was still angry about being left behind.

Instead, I focused on putting the scene of Mr. Prater and the horse down on paper. Art had been the most fun at school. Where other young ladies would learn music and other languages, deaf were taught to copy down the real world onto paper. I had struggled with the skill of using paint for this, but charcoal was my forte.

Once I was satisfied I had captured the scene as best as I was able, I stretched my skills by creating quick sketches of my family. Perhaps I would include them in my letter to my best friend so she would know what my family looked like. I took a second look at the one I had done of Cordelia scowling and thought better of that idea.

When my hand cramped, I ended my drawing session and opened up Hamlet. More than ever I felt I understood the Prince of Denmark's struggles. The words pulled me into that world so thoroughly that it wasn't until his shadow fell on me that I realized Mr. Prater was on the porch.

His clothes were stained with some wet substance, and he had a broad, excited grin on his face. He made the sign for horse and gestured for me to come with him. Curious, I used my book as a weight to hold my sketches down and stood up. I followed him back out to the barn and the same stall.

Inside, the mare was on her feet with a wobbly foal nursing. Its hair was shiny and slick from just being born. I'd never seen anything so beautiful in my life.

After a while, I realized I was leaning against the door. I looked over to the right and met Mr. Prater's dark-eyed gaze. A blush crept its way up my neck, heating up my skin.

"Feeling better, Miss Steele?" he asked. He spoke slowly, but not in the exaggerated way most people did when they talked to me.

It was kind of him to have noticed, though I didn't think it had been a secret. My blush intensified as I remembered screaming at the sky. More than likely he'd heard that. Feeling self-conscious, I nodded. Gathering my courage, I took a deep breath.

"Ivy," I said, raising my little finger of my right hand and moving it upward in a zigzag pattern. I pointed to myself and repeated the sign that was my name. "Ivy."

He straightened up and repeated the sign. "Ivy, then."

Since I left the school in Hartford, he was the first person to use my sign name. Not even Aunt Ruth had used it, preferring to speak my name when I was watching. Blinking quickly, I fought to keep back tears. The last thing I wanted was to cry in front of Mr. Prater.

I pointed at him and mouthed, "You?"

His gaze slipped to the side for a moment, and he seemed to hesitate. " -emy," he finally said.

That made no sense. "Emy?" I asked, using my voice. I'd known a girl named Emmy at school, but I didn't think that was what he meant.

To my surprise, he laughed and shook his head. He crouched down and, using his finger, began to write in the dirt. He spelled out four letters: R-E-M-Y. Remy? His name was Remy Prater? Unusual, but much better than Emmy!

Nodding, I used my right hand to spell it out. Remy. Now that I knew his first name, I would have to decide on the sign name I would give him. In the week I had been with my family, I hadn't been able to work out what would be a good sign for each of them. Most of my ideas were on the mean side.

Remy looked over his shoulder as though he had heard something and stood up. He walked to the barn door and lifted his hand in greeting. I turned back to watching the newborn foal.

A short time later and Simon was beside me. When I glanced over, he had the biggest grin on his face. In fact, it was the happiest I had seen him since I'd arrived.

For several moments, we stood side by side and watched the foal try out his legs. Impulsively, I reached out, wrapped my arms around his arm, and leaned against him. He didn't try to shake me off, which was a significant improvement in my opinion.

It didn't last.

Anna rushed up to Simon's other side and grabbed his arm. He shook us both off, and I didn't blame him. He wasn't something to be fought over like a toy.

"I want to name it," Anna said, her hands clapping together. "Can I pet it?"

"No," Simon responded. In the stall, the new mother horse eyed us with suspicion.

"But Si—"

Disgusted by her begging, I pulled away from the stall door. That's when I remembered my sketches. I'd left them on the porch, right where anyone could see them. Panicked, I rushed out of the barn and started for the house. Cordelia was nowhere in sight, but Father was at the foot of the porch steps with Remy.

For a moment, I thought my stepmother must have found my sketches and taken them with her. But then, I saw that Remy had his hands behind his back, and in his right hand was my book with my papers stuck inside it. My gaze went to the porch floor, and I saw my charcoal pencils resting by steps where I had left them.

Not caring how he managed to do it, I passed behind Remy and snatched the book from him. He didn't even glance my way as he continued to talk to Father. I bent down and retrieved my pencils as I went up onto the porch.

Cordelia confronted me in the doorway, visibly angry. She pointed back. "Where is—" I lost whatever she was asking about, and frankly I didn't care.

"I did the dishes. What more did you expect of me? You left me no instructions," my hand movements were sharp, conveying my anger. I didn't even mouth the words for her. "I disobeyed nothing. You have no reason to be angry with me."

With that, I walked to the ladder. If Cordelia thought she was going to control my life, she was mistaken.

Chapter Ten

Smiling while I did whatever my stepmother ordered me to do only seemed to annoy her. Maybe she expected me to be miserable, but I could hide what I was feeling the same as anyone else. It was satisfying to annoy her, as bad as that might sound.

Each day was the same as the previous two weeks: washing, mending, ironing, cleaning, and weeding the garden. Susan, for whatever reason, took over gathering eggs in the morning. At the very least, Cordelia didn't put all the chores on me and leave nothing to her children.

What I hated the most was when my stepmother would order me to change or dress the toddlers. Sam loathed me on sight, wanting Cordelia and no one else, and he would scream. I couldn't hear it, but the sight of his bright red, tear-stained face was more than I could take. Oddly enough, Katie appeared to have warmed up to me, though, smiling every time she saw me.

How soon before there was a new baby? I wanted to ask, but I doubted Anna and Cordelia would tell me.

Two weeks more passed with each day like the previous weekdays had been. Every Sunday, I was left behind because "it was easier" for me. It was a stupid reason, and though I think they knew it, it was the only one they gave me.

Did Father know what she was doing? What did she have to gain by isolating me? I couldn't leave because where would I go and how would I have the money to get there? Did she like the tension, the fighting? I certainly didn't.

One Sunday, as I sat on the porch steps with my sketchbook, I realized I'd been in Montana for a month. I was no closer to my brother or father, and I didn't know how I would be able to do so.

As I brushed at my eyes, Remy came up to me. A frown on his face, he settled down beside me. It was the second time he'd stayed behind on a Sunday, and I briefly wondered what had kept him on the ranch this time. Managing a wobbly smile, I faced him. Why did he always find me when I was an emotional mess?

"What's wrong?" he asked.

I shook my head, which he didn't seem to like. It was just too hard to explain. His gaze dropped to my sketches, and he raised his eyebrows. He reached over and asked, "May I?"

For a moment, I hesitated. I'd never showed anyone my sketches, besides my art teacher at school. What would be the harm, though? I handed him the leather portfolio that contained my work. He took off his hat and set it on the step next to himself.

I watched him as he flipped through the pages. I'd tried to sketch some of my memories from my journey across the country since I hadn't had my paper and pencils at the time. The most recent ones, the ones I'd just drawn, were on top, and pictures from earlier in the year were on the bottom.

Not for the first time, I wondered why Remy was so nice to me. Did he feel sorry for me? I wouldn't have been surprised if he did. I felt sorry for myself.

Too late, I realized which sketch he had in his hand. I reached to take it from him, but he held it out of reach. He looked from the paper to me with a frown. "Did this happen?"

The sketch was a third person view of Uncle Richard and myself, but no one but me would know it. In the picture, the man was holding my wrist, keeping me from getting away. His other hand was upraised as though he was about to strike.

Desperately, I tried to take it from him. His frown deepening, Remy handed it to me. He didn't stop watching me as I slipped it back under the other sketches. He caught my hand, and I felt compelled to tell him what I hadn't told my family. I gave a slow nod.

His eyes darkened with anger, and he pointed at me. I nodded again. Yes, I was the girl in the sketch. For a moment, he leaned his head back and closed his eyes. Then, Remy refocused on me. "Who?" he asked.

With a sigh, I pulled the sketch back. Using my pencil, I wrote "Uncle Richard" above the man. If anything, that made the anger in Remy's eyes increase. I wrote at the top of the page "He didn't hurt me." Not seriously, anyway.

"He should not have touched you like that," Remy said each word with deliberate slowness. He was always careful to make sure I could understand him.

"Aunt Ruth stopped him most of the time." I couldn't even begin to number the times Aunt Ruth had intervened and separated me from my uncle.

"You must miss her."

I gave a nod as my gaze went to the horizon. I did miss Aunt Ruth. She'd cared for me, protected me since I was six years old and had no one else. She hadn't been openly affectionate, but I knew she loved me. Every time she had stepped between Uncle Richard and me had been proof enough.

My memories made my heart ache. Remy's hand curled around mine, making me look at him. "You will find your place."

Surprised, I stared at him as he squeezed my fingers. How did he know I felt out of place? He pulled his hand back and stood up. Wait. He couldn't just leave like that. I flipped to an empty page and quickly scribbled the question that had been on my mind.

Why do some call you Will, but you say your name is Remy?

When I held the page up for him to read, a smile appeared for a split second on his lips. He took the book and pen from me. His response took only a minute to write. As he handed me the items back, he picked up his hat. He settled it on his head and tipped it to me before he started the walk to the barn.

Disappointed our conversation was over, I turned my attention to what he had written.

My full name is William Remington Prater. My pa was called Will, and I'd prefer not to be known by the same name.

My mother called me Remy after her father, who came from New Orleans.

THAT NIGHT I COULDN'T sleep. I tossed and turned, my mind unable to rest. How would I find my place on the ranch when no one wanted anything to do with me? For the most part, I did everything I was told to do, and it still wasn't enough.

Giving up on sleep for the moment, I stared at the ceiling. Maybe I had no place in Montana, and it was useless for me to keep fighting. But what else could I do? I had nowhere to go and no way to get there even if I did. I had some skills, especially with sewing, but who would take on a deaf girl from nowhere?

Wonderful. Negative thoughts and I couldn't stop from thinking them.

Before long, I realized light was coming up from downstairs. Father had been working on the account books when I'd climbed the ladder for bed. Was he still at work on them? My curiosity got the better of me, and I got up. Wrapping my shawl around my shoulders, I went to the ladder and climbed downstairs.

Sure enough, Father was still at the table, the lamp burning beside him. The account book was in front of him, and the pen was in his hand. Father was slumped over with his head pillowed on his arm, fast asleep. With a smile, I tiptoed over to look over his shoulder. He hadn't finished the figures.

With gentleness and care, I took the pen from his hand before it managed to blot over anything significant. Next,

I slid the book out from under his arm. Father shifted but didn't wake up. Relieved, I sat down and began to study the numbers. Everything was written neatly.

I glanced at Father and came to a quick decision. I dipped the pen in the open ink bottle and got to work. Working with numbers came easily for me. They made sense when little else did.

It didn't take me long to add the numbers up, and when I was done, I knew why Father had made the decision not to send me back to Hartford. The majority of his customers had outstanding balances they hadn't paid. It was nature of business, I knew, but this was worrying. No wonder Father always looked tired and concerned! How had he managed to keep sending me to school in the first place?

How had Cordelia not known all these years? And why hadn't Father explained this to me earlier? I would have understood and knowing the reason made it easier to accept, even if I wished circumstances were different.

I closed the book and set it in place in front of Father. Then, I capped the ink. Though I debated waking him, I decided it would be best to leave him where he was. From the rocking chair in front of the fireplace, I grabbed a quilt and carried it over. I draped it over Father's shoulders so he wouldn't get cold.

Glad I had been able to help, even in that small way, I returned to the attic. Anna and Susan didn't move, so I must have kept quiet enough not to disturb them. As I crawled under the quilt on my bed, I wondered if Father would let me help him keep his books in the future. He didn't enjoy doing it, and I liked numbers.

And, just maybe, I could do it at the general store so he wouldn't have to bring it home. That would get me off the ranch.

Hopefully, I would find some way of asking him.

OVER BREAKFAST, FATHER thanked Simon for doing the books and making it easier for him. My brother just blinked and shook his head. "Wasn't me, Pa," he said. In turn, Cordelia and Anna also denied having done it.

Father looked puzzled but dropped the matter. He didn't even ask if it had been me. I could have spoken up, but drawing attention to it seemed like it would make a mountain out of a molehill. Biting my cheek to keep from smiling, I dropped my gaze to my food. When I happened to glance up, Remy was staring at me.

Had he guessed the truth?

Cordelia gestured for me to help clear the table with Susan, so I had no opportunity to approach Father about my idea. Anna started the water heating on the stove for the laundry. The house began to warm up as the steam filled the air.

My step-sister piled dirty laundry in the yard next to the washtub. To my surprise, as soon as she dropped the clothing and sheets, Anna went back to the house. Susan didn't come out, and neither did Cordelia.

They expected, without actually saying it, me to do the laundry alone. Gritting my teeth, I got to work. Whenever I filled a basket with clean, wet laundry, I had to carry it to the line and pin it up to dry. I had barely made a dent in the task when a familiar cowboy approached me.

When Remy offered his hand to me, I didn't hesitate to take it, though I dried my hand on my skirt before I did. He led me to the newly repaired corral where a massive black horse paced back and forth. I could feel the pounding of his hoofs against the ground as I drew closer. Where had this animal come from?

Releasing my hand, Remy climbed through the rails, entering the corral. What was he doing? Why would he get in there with that beast? He could get hurt! He glanced over his shoulder and offered a quick grin. Then he focused on the horse.

I clasped the top rail, my anxiety rising as I watched. Every step he took was slow, and he held his hands out. He reminded me of some of my teachers when they would console someone frightened at school. He stance was non-threatening and calm. As concerned as I was, I couldn't help but be fascinated.

The horse stamped its feet and tossed its head. It—he?—bolted to the far side of the corral. Remy came to a halt and turned his back on the animal.

My eyes must have been as round as dinner plates as I looked on. My heartfelt as though it was in my throat and I held my breath. Remy dared to wink at me as he remained completely still.

After several minutes, when I thought nothing was going to happen, the horse shook its head. Not in the wild manner as before, but more in a curious way. Perhaps he was as confused about Remy's behavior as I was. It took one step and, after a pause, another. Slowly, yet surely, it walked up behind the young cowboy.

The horse nudged Remy's shoulder as though offended about being ignored. In a slow, careful manner, Remy turned and began stroking the horse's neck.

I'd never seen anything like it.

Remy curled his fingers around the halter and led the creature to where I was. Amazed and just a bit terrified, I stared at the magnificent animal. I couldn't stop myself from taking a step back. What was to prevent the horse from breaking the boards that made up the corral?

"No need to be afraid," Remy said, a full-fledged grin on his face. At least with him, I never felt like he was laughing at me. He reached out his hand across the corral. "Don't be scared."

Unsure what he intended to do, I returned to the fence. He took my hand and brought it up toward the horse. I flinched right before I felt the velvety soft nose. The horse snorted as I tentatively stroked its nose and it nibbled at my fingers, searching for some food.

All of a sudden, it jerked back, and Remy released the halter to avoid getting dragged away. I twisted around to see what had startled the horse and it wasn't hard to miss Anna, who was running towards us. She must have called out something.

"What are you doing?" she asked as she reached the corral.

"Don't do that again! ....know better!" His eyes glinted with a controlled annoyance as he came through the corral fence.

Anna took a step back, apparently not accustomed to being scolded. She glanced at me and her expression hardened. She spun on her heel and walked away, which was not what I expected her to do.

I sent a confused look towards Remy, but he wasn't looking at me. I ducked my head and started back towards the house. I'd been away from the washing for long enough.

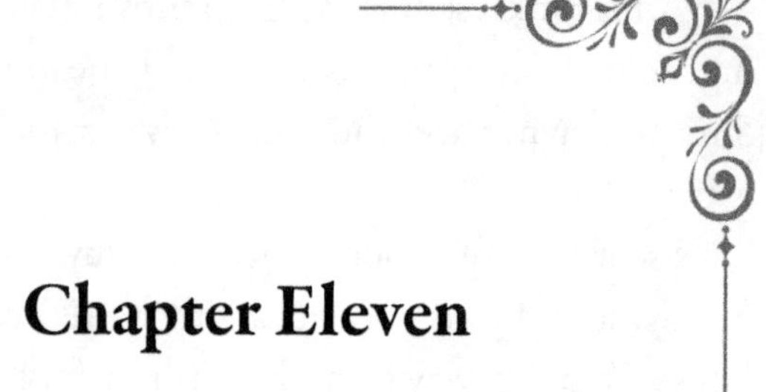

Chapter Eleven

By Wednesday, I was on the verge of exhaustion. I couldn't remember a week when I'd worked harder. I'd done all the wash alone on Monday and on Tuesday, I had faced the ironing alone. Cordelia and Anna were involved in some sewing project they had begun.

My temper had reached its limit, and when my step-mother ordered me to start the mending, I was done. They already had their fabric laid out on the table, evidence that they were continuing the dress they were putting together.

"No." I didn't care if my pitch or tone of voice was grating when I spoke. She couldn't pretend she didn't understand me.

"I didn't ask, Ivy," she said, her eyes narrowing. "I will tell—"

"My father?" I signed and mouthed at the same time. "Go ahead. In case you didn't know, slavery was abolished years ago." Then, to make sure she completely understood me, I said, "I am not your slave."

All color drained out of Cordelia's face, and she took a step back. "How dare you!"

I wasn't sure which of my words had offended her so much unless it was my continued refusal to do as she said, but I did not back down. I was more than happy to do my share, but she had no right to put every hard task on me.

Her lips trembled, and she spun away. She ran into the bedroom and closed the door. The next thing I knew, Anna was in my face. "Why did you say that?" she asked, her blue eyes sparkling with anger.

Words cannot describe just how much I did not like having people invade my personal space. I lifted my hands and pushed her back. "Why not? It was the truth!" I signed, not bothering with mouthing the words. I was in a petty frame of mind, and I was tired of always bending to their wishes.

"Stop! No one...to see you...your hands!" Anna said, flailing her hands in mockery of my signing. I had the feeling I'd missed several crucial words in her sentence. "No one cares."

Finally, someone had said it. "Do you think I don't know that?" My hands moved in sharp, blunt movements. Again, I made the deliberate decision not to mouth the words. "You and your mother have made that as clear as crystal, but I'm not going anywhere."

Anna turned her head, and she suddenly had a smile on her face. I followed her gaze and saw the children in the doorway. Susan had Sam in her arms and Katie was just behind her. They looked worried. "Where's Ma?" Susan asked

Even I knew better than to argue in front of them. I turned my back on Anna and went to the mending pile. While I wasn't going to do it all myself, I wouldn't completely neglect the task either.

As I threw myself into the task, my anger leached away, leaving me even more tired than before. It wasn't fair that I had to fight to be treated like everyone else and I always had the same question at the back of my mind: would things be different if I weren't deaf?

Would Father have told his new wife he had a daughter in the east? Or would I have come west when he and Simon did? Would Cordelia be more accepting of me if she'd known about me before I arrived?

There were so many different ways, different choices in life. I couldn't help but think one of them would have been better.

CORDELIA, FOR SOME unknown reason, did not tell Father about my insubordination. At least, he didn't scold me for being disrespectful that or any other night. I decided to be glad about it and not let it bother me.

My step-sister, on the other hand, made it clear she was angry with me. Whenever we made eye contact, she would glare and then turn her back on me. What had I said that had so offended her?

There were no pleasant interludes with Remy. I'd finally worked out a sign for him and couldn't wait to show him. In the process, I'd also created sign names for Simon and Susan, though they hadn't seemed to notice.

One Friday morning, the routine changed without any warning. Anna and Cordelia, along with Simon, had been gathering sharp knives and every pot or bucket on the ranch. Then, Simon herded the lone fat, slow pig out of the barn. Curious and confused about what was happening, I drew closer.

Then, as I saw Simon heft a hatchet, I realized what was going to happen. I couldn't bear to see my brother kill the animal and I spun away. My deafness kept me from hearing the final blow, which was a relief.

Dressed in her oldest dress, no doubt so that it did not matter if blood stained it or not, Anna pushed past me. I dared to glance over my shoulder, and sure enough, the hog was dead.

The scarlet blood caught my attention followed by that distinct metallic scent on the breeze. I gagged, my mind going back to the last few times I'd had occasion to smell blood: the poor man who'd been shot on the stage, and the butcher's shop the day I found Aunt Ruth dead. It was not a smell that boded any good.

Clapping my hand over my mouth, I knew I couldn't stay in the yard and began to back up. I'd only gone a few steps, and I saw Cordelia turn my way. She made an impatient gesture for me to join them, but I couldn't make myself move forward.

She must have said something when she faced away from me because Anna spun around. Maybe it was because she was mad at me already, but right as I saw that she held a bucket in her hand, she tossed the contents at me.

Blood sailed through the air. My breath caught in my throat as I jerked back. Most of the still warm liquid missed me, but a good portion splashed onto my skirt. Appalled, I stared at the dripping blood.

Why? Why did she hate me so much?

When I looked up, Simon had grabbed Anna's arm, and it seemed as though he were yelling at her. Tears welled in my eyes, though, and I didn't stick around to see what happened next. My blood-soaked skirt clung to my legs as I ran from the yard.

Only one thought was in my mind: I had to get rid of that blood.

There was a small lake, not far from the house. I'd only been there once when Remy had shown me where it was. The surface of the water glittered and sparkled in the sunlight. I fell on my knees by the edge. At first, I plunged the fabric into the cold water and scrubbed at it. It didn't seem to be enough.

Desperation tinged my emotions, and I twisted my arms back to undo all the buttons. Somehow, I managed to free myself and pulled the entire gown over my head. I plunged the whole thing into the water.

How fortunate that I was far from everything because I was left in just my chemise, corset, and bloomers. As I rubbed at the fabric, I prayed that Remy wouldn't come and find me. Being an emotional mess was one thing, but to be found in my underclothes would be something I would not be able to live down.

Despite my efforts, the fabric of my blue calico dress remained stained. My frantic movements slowed to nothing as I gave it up as useless. I leaned back and closed my eyes. Anna must have known this would happen, but she'd done it anyway.

A hand on my shoulder made me open my eyes with a start. It was Simon who stood over me, an expression of concern on his face. Once he was sure he had my attention, he began to unbutton his shirt. He pulled the garment off and handed it to me.

I suppose finding one's sister in a state of undress would prompt one to find some way to cover her. With a half smile, I took the shirt and wrapped it around my shoulders.

Crouching beside me, Simon lifted my waterlogged dress and shook his head. He glanced at me, his brown eyes sad. "I'm sorry."

"You didn't do this," I signed, feeling tired. How long would I be able to stay away from the ranch? I was sure I would not be ready to face seeing the blood again. Would Anna and Cordelia take care of the pig alone?

To my surprise, Simon took a seat. His knees bent, he rested his elbows on them. He stared out at the surface of the lake, and it seemed as though he wasn't going anywhere. After a few minutes, he turned his head towards me.

"What were you reminded of?" he asked, curiosity shining through the sadness.

Using my finger, I wrote in the damp sand: Aunt Ruth. My brother nodded and then asked, "Do...know why Pa is...here?"

Wait. Did he mean to ask why Father was here, as in the Montana territory or the ranch? Or had I missed part of what he said, and he meant to ask why our father was not on the ranch? In any event, I just shook my head.

Simon's shoulders rose and fell with a sigh. "Blood makes him sick too."

I'd just assumed that Father had no part because he was busy in town with running the general store, but now that I thought about it, what Simon said made sense.

How much blood and suffering Father must have seen in the war. If I was affected by the smell, and my experiences had been brief, I couldn't imagine just how much he must detest blood. It was hard to believe he'd come all this way, into the rough west. Undoubtedly, he must have encountered more fighting and more blood since he'd taken up living in the territory.

Shaking my head, I refocused on my brother. With a flinch, I realized he'd kept talking while I wasn't looking. "—be away until late." He tossed a pebble at the water. "I should get back and help."

Was that a hint that I needed to return as well? Wishing I'd paid attention and learned something more about my father, I heaved a sigh and moved to stand up. Simon put his hand on my arm, though, and stopped me.

He shook his head and got to his feet. "Stay," he said, looking down at me. "I don't think you will be much help anyway."

That was true, and I gave a brief nod. Simon walked away, leaving me on the edge of the water. Leaning my head back, I watched as birds swooped overhead. It was one of the few times I felt at peace.

Inevitably, my thoughts went to Anna's actions. One way or another, we were going to have to find some way to get along. We couldn't talk it out since she had no patience for me to write out my answers.

Sighing, I closed my eyes.

"I THINK IVY SHOULD come with us tomorrow."

When I glanced up while at the dinner table on Saturday night, I had not expected to see Anna say those words. I wasn't the only one to stare at her in surprise. Nothing had changed between us in three days, but now she was suddenly on my side? Why? What did she have to gain by it?

"Anna, I don't think—" Cordelia started to say.

"Think about it," Anna interrupted. I didn't like the smile that curved her lips. "How will she marry well if she doesn't meet anyone? She needs to be seen."

Marriage? When had marriage ever come into it? And who was interested in me? I was so mixed up by what was going on I couldn't feel happy about how much easier it had gotten to read their lips. When there were only six people in my life, I learned how their mouth moved for each word. It wasn't like I had anything else to do.

Remy frowned. He looked just as bothered by the suggestion as I felt. He wasn't the only one, either. Everyone was talking, and I couldn't keep up with them all

"I don't think...necessary," Father said, his expression concerned. Simon said something at the same time which I missed altogether.

"Anna ...not be cruel." This came from Cordelia, who sent a worried glance at me. For a moment, I was caught between confusion and offense. Why did Cordelia think the idea of me getting married was cruel?

"Well, you don't...she will stay here forever, can she?" Anna pointed out. Her expression had become smug. "In fact, I know someone...might have an interest in her."

"Let's discuss this another time, Anna." Cordelia looked annoyed with her daughter.

"I don't...Ivy wants to rush into...," Father said, a frown creasing his forehead. He looked wholly unsettled by the idea of me marrying. What had he expected for my future?

I felt the tabletop jerk and, when everyone turned their heads towards the bottom of the table, I followed their gazes to Remy. Both of his hands were flat on the table as though he'd slammed them down. "Let Ivy have a choice in the matter," he said.

Surprised expressions on their faces, the rest of the family moved their gazes to me. My cheeks heated up with a blush at their sudden scrutiny. Had they forgotten I was there or did they think they would know what was best for me?

"What do...want, Ivy?" Remy asked.

Did he mean to ask did I want to be married? It wasn't a specific question, or at least, I didn't have an exact answer. I hadn't thought of marriage as anything more than something that would happen in time. There was, however, one desire I did have.

"I want to go to town," I signed, mouthing only the last word of my sentence.

"What did she say?" Cordelia asked, her expression frustrated.

To my surprise, it wasn't Remy who answered her. Cordelia's head twisted to the right, to where Simon was sitting on her left. "—to go with us," my brother said. He had a half smile on his face as though the whole thing amused him. "She wants to go to church."

Cordelia's face showed alarm, though Father nodded. "That...that," he said, reaching for the bowl of mashed potatoes. "I don't think anything else need be said."

"We should—" Whatever my step-mother intended to say, she was cut off by my father, though I missed what he said. Cordelia dropped her gaze to her plate and remained silent.

While I knew I should be concerned about what kind of repercussions my step-mother would come up with over this, I couldn't keep my excitement down. Thanks to Anna and Remy, I was going to leave the ranch!

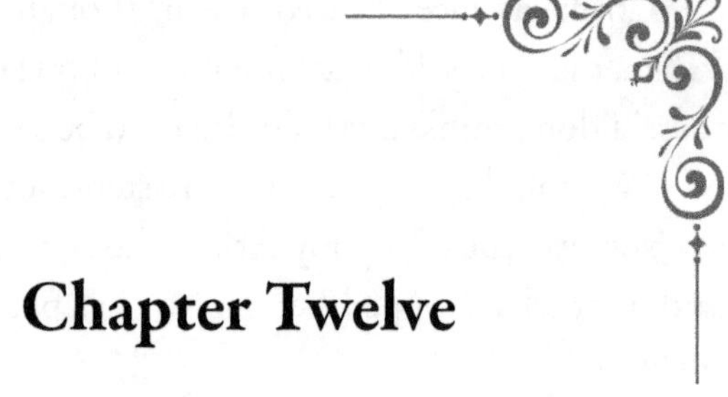

Chapter Twelve

The next morning, my fingers trembled when I dressed the next morning. When I'd gone to bed, it had been hard to miss how Cordelia and Father argued by the fireplace. I could only hope that my step-mother hadn't convinced Father that my going to church was a bad idea.

Breakfast had an air of tension as we all ate. Cordelia encouraged everyone to eat quickly, no doubt so there would be time for the dishes to be done before we left. Susan, still sleepy, earned a swat to the back of the head for taking too long. My step-mother used the time to pack food into a basket.

I was the first one to climb into the back of the wagon, and Simon laughed at my eagerness. He, as he had every other Sunday, had chosen to ride his horse instead of joining the rest of the family. That was something I'd noticed as of late. Though Simon was friendly with his step-siblings and affectionate with Katie and Sam, he kept a distance from them whenever he could.

Maybe it was just his personality to keep others at bay, and he didn't resent my arrival as I'd thought at first.

As most of the days had been since I'd arrived, it was sunny out. Simon and Remy rode ahead of the wagon. To my surprise, Katie insisted on using my lap as her seat, screaming when her sister tried to take her away. She spent the entire drive tracing the embroidery on my skirt. Anna kept glancing at us, open jealousy on her face.

I made a mental tally. With Susan tolerating me, Katie enamored with my dress, Simon amused by me, and Sam too little to have an opinion, I had made a start at winning over my family. Of course, that left the hardest members of the family for me to work out how not to be on their bad side.

How difficult could it be?

There were only a few people I recognized in the churchyard when Father brought the wagon to a halt. Unfortunately, one of them was the strange man who'd been so eager to meet me the last time I had been to church: John Dover. He came towards the wagon, pulling his hat off.

Stepping in front of the man, Remy reached up to help me down. Looking over Remy's shoulder, I saw Dover scowl, but in the next moment, he had a smile on his face. If there was anything I knew not to trust, it was a person who could change his expressions so fast.

Putting a polite smile on my life, I gave Mr. Dover a quick nod and hurried to follow my father. Was he the man Anna believed was interested in marrying me? Why? He knew nothing about me, and I only knew his name. True, some marriages had begun with nothing more, but that was not how I wanted to go about things.

If I married, I wanted to know the man who would be my husband and be sure he wouldn't hold my deafness against me. He would have to be someone who would be understanding and would face the challenges a deaf wife would undoubtedly bring.

My eyes drifted to where Remy was surrounded by other people, Anna among them. The expression on his face was one of annoyance and impatience. He must not enjoy being the center of attention, which was something I could relate to.

Several of the ladies I passed quickly averted their eyes. I couldn't help but wonder what they had been told about me. Before I could follow that train of thought to what would only be a bitter conclusion, Sheriff Worth stepped in front of me.

"Miss Ivy," he greeted, tipping his hat. In his other hand was a poster. His mustache —had he always had that or was it new?— made it slightly difficult, but not impossible, to read his lips. "I hoped ...see you...soon."

My curiosity piqued, I tilted my head. Why would he want to speak to me? I hadn't done a thing wrong in my life. To my surprise, Father and Cordelia didn't even pause. In fact, all of my family went their own way.

"Does this man look familiar?" he asked, and then held up the poster.

It was a wanted poster, something I'd seen a lot more of after I crossed the Mississippi. I reached out and took the poster from the sheriff to examine the sketch closer. There weren't many details contained in the sketch. The man portrayed seemed to be slender and clean-shaven. His nose was narrow, and he had high cheekbones. None of these features looked familiar, so I shifted my attention to the writing.

James Jones AKA "Black Jim" was wanted for highway robbery and murder. There was a reward of five hundred dollars in gold for the man to be brought in dead or alive.

For an instant, I wondered if it would be enough money to get me back East. Maybe, but I had nothing left for me there since it certainly wasn't enough to get me back into school. In any event, as far as I could remember, I had never seen the man on the poster before.

Sorry I couldn't be more help, I shook my head and handed it back. The disappointment on Sheriff Worth's face was palpable, but he nodded. He folded the poster and slipped it in his pocket. "Thank you."

Wait. Why had he shown me that? He started to turn away, but I waved my hand to get his attention. "Why?" I mouthed and signed at the same time, hoping he would understand.

His shoulders rose and fell with a sigh, so I assumed he understood. He glanced around as though he wanted to make sure no one was nearby. "Sheriff Bar...believes this man...part of the gang that stopped your stage."

Sheriff Bar? Oh, Sheriff Barrington who I'd given my description to after the robbery. I hadn't thought much about the robbers since I'd arrived. Had another stagecoach been stopped? I wanted to ask, but I could see everyone in the yard moving to the church door.

The sheriff tipped his hat and turned. As I walked to the front of the church, I tried to catch up to my family. I was thankful to find them in the second to last pew and to see that they had left me enough room to sit on the end. Too late did I realize it had been planned, by Anna no doubt.

Mr. Dover leaned over and gestured for me to make room for him. Alarmed, I stared up at him. Surely, there was somewhere else for him to sit! He motioned with his hand again, this time with more impatience.

As I remembered how angry Cordelia had been about the incident with the squirrel, I didn't want to risk being forbidden from coming into town. I slid over, pressing against my brother as much as I could. Simon moved over, giving me a confused look until he realized why I had moved.

His face darkened, and my brother stared at Mr. Dover. When everyone rose for the first hymn, Simon grabbed my shoulders and switched places with me. That put me between him and Anna, who frowned at me. She refused to allow me any more room, and because Simon made sure to keep a little space between himself and Mr. Dover, I felt cramped.

I refused to glance in Mr. Dover's direction to see what he made of the switch. His opinion was of no concern to me, and I hoped that he would take the hint that I had no interest in his attention.

THOUGH I UNDERSTOOD nothing of the reverend's sermon, again, I was happy I was there. I glanced around the congregation and tried to find one person to meet. That was the first way to make friends, wasn't it? Steeling my nerves, I hoped Cordelia wouldn't insist on leaving immediately.

When the last prayer was said—and again Anna elbowed me when I didn't lower my head—I wasn't pushed towards the door. Anna may have tried to make me move, but

Simon refused to take a step. Fortunately, someone in the next pew started a conversation with Father and Cordelia, so they didn't notice.

It was hard to tell if Simon was talking to Mr. Dover or not since he stood with his back to me. Had he gone into protective, older brother mode? The idea warmed my heart.

After a minute, Mr. Dover put his hat on his head and walked away from the pew. Several of the congregation were already filing out of the building, so I quickly lost sight of him. He was a strange person, and I couldn't shake the feeling of mistrust in my mind.

When I glanced over my shoulder, Anna had a scowl on her face. "That was rude," she said, though I couldn't tell if she directed that comment towards Simon or me.

In any event, Father and Cordelia shepherded us out the door a few minutes later. Anna collected the picnic basket, and our family walked to where everyone else seemed to be congregating for one large picnic. Children ran from one spread-out blanket to another, food in hand as they tried to get the best of everything.

Simon only stayed long enough to grab some of the roast beef and bread. Then, he was off to who knew where. Anna did the same, only she remained in sight, settling on a blanket with her friends. Every few minutes, one of them would glance over in my direction, so I could only guess as to what Anna was telling them.

I hadn't decided on whom I would introduce myself to. Several ladies looked friendly enough, though I couldn't keep from feeling nervous about approaching them. Before I could make up my mind, a shadow fell onto the blanket.

When I looked up, I recognized the reverend—what was his name?— with a pretty woman on his arm. Was that his wife? I felt a little ashamed that I didn't already know.

The reverend crouched down and held out his hand. "Hello, Miss Ivy."

Delighted to meet him officially, I signed, "Nice to meet you" and then put my right hand in his. He didn't show any surprise, so someone must have told him about my deafness. His gray eyes had a kind expression in them, and I was close enough to see the lines around his eyes. I estimated his age to be somewhere around fifty years old.

His gaze shifted to Father. "I'm glad to see your entire family today."

A flush spread across Cordelia's cheeks, and she dropped her gaze. The woman who had been clinging to the reverend's arm also knelt down. "Hello," she said, moving her mouth slowly. "I am Mary. I'm pleased to meet you, Miss Ivy."

Again, I signed, "Nice to meet you." Her brown eyes were kind, and now that she was closer I could see that she was not much younger than her husband. Would she be a friend much as Mrs. Weston had been in Springfield? I hoped that would be the case. She would be my first friend—besides Remy, of course—I'd made in Montana.

As the reverend and his wife spoke to Father and Cordelia, my gaze shifted to the other picnickers. I didn't see Remy anywhere and wondered if he'd gone back to the ranch. If I'd been surrounded by people as he'd been before church, I think I would have been eager to leave as well.

After a few moments, the reverend moved on to speak to others of his congregation. It was nice to see him do so since not all reverends took such an interest in others.

Mr. Dover, who stood several yards away, caught my gaze and winked at me! I turned my head away. Why did the man have such an interest in me? Though I couldn't work out the reason, I resolved not to give him any encouragement in the future and hope he would find some other girl to fix his attention on.

AFTER THAT SUNDAY, Cordelia was not as strict about how much work I had to do each day. I had time to sketch in the afternoons. Otherwise, her attitude toward me didn't change even a little. For whatever reason, she still didn't like me.

And, when a crate arrived for me from Springfield, she had reason to hate me even more.

Though I'd been careful to narrow my belongings into a single carpetbag and trunk, there had been other things I couldn't bear to part with. These I had packed carefully into a crate, and Mrs. Weston had sworn to send it after me.

When Father brought it home on Thursday afternoon, I was ecstatic. Simon helped me to pry open the top, leaving the crate on the porch. I had everyone's attention, though Cordelia and Anna tried to behave as though they didn't care, as I delved into the crate.

The first thing I drew out was a quilt I had used to protect the more fragile items within. It was one of two I knew Mama had sewn herself. When I looked over, there was a hint of recognition in Simon's eyes. Feeling generous, I held it out to him. It was only fair he possess something of our mother's just as I did.

He took the quilt from me with a slight smile. I didn't dare look over to see what Father thought of it, as much as I wanted to know if he recognized these pieces from his past.

In any event, the next thing I pulled out from the straw was the first teacup of my mother's china set. I was delighted and surprised to see that it hadn't been damaged during transport, though it had the slightest chip on the handle.

Simon's hand took it from mine, and when I glanced over, he had a grin on his face. At the same time, tears made his eyes glisten. "Mama loved these," he said. If I'd had any doubt about whether he missed our mother or not, now I didn't.

I saw him flinch and when I turned my head, I realized that the front door was closed and Cordelia wasn't on the porch anymore. I felt a sliver of guilt at reminding her of her predecessor, but I had a mother I loved dearly even if she had died so long ago.

The next thing that I removed from the crate was the family shelf clock, amazed to see its hands still for the first time. It had sat in my room in Springfield since Father and Simon left, and before that, I could remember how it sat above the fireplace in our home. Father had made sure it kept the right time every week.

It was something that was to be enjoyed and didn't belong to me. I'd only taken custody of it. Taking a deep breath, I turned to where Father was still by the porch steps, and his face held no expression. I held the clock out to him.

After a moment, Father shook his head and pushed it back towards me. "We have Cordelia's clock."

Cordelia's clock was a large grandfather that stood next to the front door. But why couldn't we set the shelf clock by the fireplace? Just because there was already a clock in the house didn't mean the clock that had been in the Steele family should be hidden away.

It wasn't as if this had been only Mama's.

Since I'd come into the house, I'd had the feeling that most of the decorations, dishes, furniture, and such all came from Cordelia, almost as though she had laid claim to the household and didn't want there to be any question about it. It wasn't fair. When two families came together, shouldn't they combine their belongings and become a new family unit?

Maybe that was too much to hope for.

I hugged the clock and turned back to my crate. The exchange had dampened my happiness, that was for sure. Most of this would be consigned to the barn with my trunk, and that's where I'd have to go if I wanted to see it.

While my back had been turned, Katie had apparently decided she didn't want to wait for me and was trying to get into the crate. She was on her tiptoes and peering over the edge of the container, which was almost as tall as she was. It was adorable and, much to my surprise, it was Remy who pulled the toddler away.

I hadn't even realized he'd joined my audience.

There wasn't much interesting left in the box. There were my other books, most of them ones I'd studied at school and a jewelry box with nothing in it. I blushed when I pulled my crinoline hoop from the crate, and I didn't dare glance at anyone as I set it aside.

At the bottom was an item I'd gone back and forth about keeping. Aunt Ruth had given it to me right after Father left, no doubt in the hopes it would cheer me up. The porcelain head and limbs of the doll were as pristine as the day I'd put it in the crate. My aunt had made the tiny blue dress that was still on the toy.

I felt a tug on my skirt. Katie had a grip on the fabric with her right hand, and she reached up with her left hand. She wanted my doll.

My first instinct was to keep it away from her. She was little and careless and wouldn't know to handle it with care. The hopeful, eager expression in her eyes, though...I couldn't resist, and I handed it to her. I was too old for dolls anyway.

Katie grinned and jumped and down. She spun and ran to Anna, holding up the doll. My step-sister forced a smile and nodded, but when Katie ran to each person to show off her new toy, Anna's face twisted with anger.

Did she think she was the only one allowed to give our half-sister something nice?

She was the only one who seemed upset. Father and Simon both had slight smiles on their faces. Remy gave me a nod, which warmed my heart even more than the approval of my parent and brother. If I was going to worry about making anyone happy, it would be those three.

Chapter Thirteen

Simon, do you know why Papa refuses to send me back to school?

It was too big of a question—the answer too important to me—for me to try to convey with my hands. I watched my brother's shoulders rise and fall with a sigh as he read my words and he shook his head. His gaze shifted to the lake in front of us.

Two weeks had passed in relative peace without any significant change. My step-mother's behavior towards me remained cool and distant. Katie became my little shadow, which was just like a toddler to become attached to someone because they give them a toy.

My relationship with Simon had improved since my crate of belongings had arrived. Maybe reminding him of our shared loss had been the key. He kept our mother's quilt on the foot of his bed, and he had begun teasing me in small ways. He'd tug my braid as if I were a child as he walked past, or he would bump my shoulder if he came up next to me.

He was the one who had suggested—through a somewhat comical display of charades—we come out to the lake. I'd brought my sketchbook, and shown my sketches to him.

He'd scrutinized them, but his expression had given little away about what he thought of them.

It was paper from my sketchbook that I used to ask my question. He reached over and took the pencil from me. As I watched, he wrote his response with care, pausing every few words to look out over the surface of the water. The fact that he was taking so long worried me.

Trying to relax, I breathed in the scent of pine and leaned my head back. The sky was a brilliant blue, and there were no clouds to hide the sun. As I watched, two rather large birds soared overhead, but they weren't close enough for me to recognize what type they were. I felt a sliver of envy at how they seemed to glide with no effort through the air.

The year before, at this same time, I would have been rushing around with my head down, hoping to avoid Uncle Richard's notice. All my focus would have been on getting through the summer with the prospect of school ahead of me.

Although I was steadily becoming content with where I was, I still felt the need to know why I couldn't go back to school.

A touch on my arm brought my focus back to where I was. Simon handed me the paper, his expression serious. Taking a deep breath, I turned my attention to the words on the page.

Pa thinks I should have the chance to further my education. Cordelia's convinced him that, as a man, I would have more benefit than you. She says that in eight years you must have learned all it's possible for someone like you to learn.

My breath caught in my throat. So it had been my step-mother's fault. I'd suspected, but it still hurt to learn she did not think I deserved the chance to learn all I could. Someone like you. Did she think that because I was deaf, I couldn't learn to enjoy things such as literature or art? Or did she think a young woman had no business learning Latin or mathematics?

It seemed every time I turned around I had more reasons to dislike Cordelia. Did that make me a bad person?

Before I could think about it, I glanced at Simon. As badly as I missed school, I wouldn't feel as bad about not going back if it was something my brother wanted. He stared at the water, his fingers drumming on his knees. He appeared restless, and a suspicion wormed its way into my mind. Grabbing the pencil, I wrote: Do you want to go?

Tapping his arm to get his attention, I held the paper up when he glanced over. His lips quirked into a slight smile and he shook his head. He took the paper and pencil from me and began to write once again. This time it didn't take him long to put his response down.

No. I want to stay in Montana and run a ranch. I don't need more education to do that. I know everything I need to make a success.

My next question was: Did you tell Father?

His answer was the one I expected: I tried.

Was he busy at the time? Maybe you should try again.

Simon raised his eyebrows and shook his head. Right. It had been a stupid thought. If Simon didn't want to go East, why couldn't I? If we could make Father understand that Simon didn't want any part of Cordelia's grand plan, would he be willing to let me go back to the life I loved?

While it might have made sense, I had the feeling it wouldn't be as simple as that. It was too late to make the journey back. It would be next to impossible to make it in time for the beginning of the semester. Even if I did, I would have to make a firm decision about what I intended for my future, because it would be costly to send me back to school only to have me return after just a couple more years. And where would I go during the holiday breaks? I could already guess what Father, and Cordelia would say to that.

What would be the point?

Cordelia had already made it clear she thought I'd had enough education, for a girl and a deaf person. I also knew just how much she influenced my father's thinking.

My head ached as I tried to work it all out in my mind. Tapping my pencil, I hesitated with my next question. Why does Anna hate me?

Simon laughed when he read that. Why wouldn't she be jealous? Up until now, she has been the princess of the family. Why would anyone look at her when there's someone cheerful and pretty right beside her?

Was that all? Was she jealous? Wait. Simon thought I was pretty? My brother had his eyes closed, his face towards the sun. With a sigh, I gave up on trying to understand my stepfamily and closed my eyes as well.

After a few minutes, I felt Simon move beside me, and I opened my eyes to see what had caught his attention. My brother was standing and looking off to the west. I leaned forward to look around him.

A horse and rider were coming toward us. I squinted to get a better look and recognized it as Remy. Quickly, I stood up. Simon raised his hand and, I assumed, called out a greeting.

"Hello," I saw Remy say as he pulled to a stop a few yards away from us. He swung out of the saddle and let the reins fall to the ground. The brown horse shook its head before it began to graze. "Nice day."

I couldn't keep the smile from my face. It felt as though it had been months since I'd last been in the cowboy's company in any private way. He sent a slight smile at me and then his gaze went to Simon. Remy gave a nod to whatever my brother said.

They continued to have a conversation, and I let my gaze go to the horse. Though it wasn't as tall as the wild ones I'd seen Remy work with, it still seemed intimidating, even as it nibbled at the grass. What made people so eager to get on the animals' backs? Why did it not run away? The reins were not tied to anything.

Remy stepped into my line of sight, facing me directly. "Do...like her?"

So, the creature was a female. Remy reached over, grabbed the reins from the ground, and brought the horse closer to me. I took a step back. "You don't have to be scared," Remy said, speaking the words slowly. "She won't hurt you." He stared at me for a moment. "Have you ever been on a horse?"

How had he guessed? I shook my head, feeling the burn of embarrassment spreading across my cheeks. It wasn't my fault I didn't know how to ride, I knew, but it somehow felt like a failure to admit it.

Simon spun around to face me as if he suddenly realized what was going on. "You can't ride?" he asked, astonishment written all over his face.

My embarrassment shifted to annoyance, and I glared at him. How, or when, did he expect me to have learned?

A hand waved, catching my attention, and I turned back to Remy. He had a smile on his face as if he found it all amusing. He gestured for me to come over to him. "There...first time for everything," he said.

Wait. He wanted me to get on his horse?

Emphatically, I shook my head. Simon, though, grabbed my arms and pushed me forward. Was it so shameful to have a sister who didn't ride that he wanted me to rectify the mistake as soon as possible?

How I wished we were alone so I could smack him as he deserved to be hit.

As it was, I found myself inches from the horse's face. Her warm breath hit my cheeks, and I couldn't resist wrinkling up my nose at the scent of grass and grain. It wasn't unpleasant, merely unexpected.

Remy took my hand and, with a gentleness that surprised me but was wholly in character for what I'd seen in him, placed my hand against the horse's nose. When I glanced over at him, I saw his lips moving, but I couldn't understand what he was saying. I could only hope his words weren't meant for me.

After a few minutes, Remy drew my hand away from the velvety soft nose to the horse's neck. He kept my hand moving in a petting motion as if trying to teach me how to do it. I would have glared at him if I wasn't so focused on just how large the horse was.

Much too soon for my taste, Remy pulled me to the horse's side. Why had he wanted me to pet the horse? Was I supposed to have made a bond or some connection with the animal? The cowboy put his hand on the stirrup.

A part of me was excited about learning something new, but a small part was terrified. And that little part was enough to keep me from moving. I felt hands on my waist, and I spun around. As hard as I could, I shoved Simon away. How dare he try to pick me and put me in the saddle!

"Sorry," Simon said, raising his hands and backing away.

When I turned back, Remy was still waiting for me. If I shook my head, if I refused, I had the feeling that he would let me. Then again, I knew he was stubborn. After all, I'd seen how persistent he could be when working with the un-broken horses that kept appearing in the corral by the barn. To back away now would only mean he would approach me again.

I may as well get it over with.

Taking a deep breath, I reached up and grabbed the saddle, as I'd seen Remy and Simon do in the past. I managed to get my foot in the stirrup, and that's as far as I would have gotten if the cowboy hadn't boosted me all the way up. The next thing I knew, I was seated in the saddle, looking down at Remy and Simon.

What was I supposed to do next?

My confusion must have shown on my face. Grinning, Remy put his hand on my leg and made sure my foot went in the stirrup. I tried to sit as I'd seen others in a saddle sit: straight and confident. The young cowboy took the reins and started to walk. The horse followed, and I grabbed the knob on the saddle to keep my balance. After a few moments, I felt sure of myself and sat up once again.

It wasn't hard to find the rhythm of the horse's pace. A grin spread across my face as Remy led the horse along the lakeside. I glanced over my shoulder to see that Simon had remained behind, for whatever reason. It was just me, Remy, and the horse.

Leaning my head back, I stared up at the birds that flew overhead. As I breathed in, I could smell a slight fishy scent coming from the lake. All the worry and stress I'd been feeling melted away as though it'd never existed.

Too soon for my taste, Remy turned to go back the way we'd come. He brought me back to where Simon was throwing rocks at the water. When the cowboy helped me to the ground, I landed a mere foot from him.

Being so close to someone didn't happen often, so I wasn't quite sure what to do. Staring at his shirt seemed rude, so I lifted my gaze. He was taller than me, but not so tall it hurt my neck to look up at him.

A slight smile played on his lips, and he brushed a lock of my hair out of my face. I hadn't even realized my hair was coming loose from the chignon at the back of my head. Though I knew I ought to step back and go to Simon, I couldn't make myself move. All I seemed capable of doing was staring into his dark eyes.

After a moment, he was the one who stepped back, a flush coloring his neck. He turned as though he intended on walking away, but then paused. I realized that I stood in the way of him mounting the horse and getting on his way. Feeling my cheeks burn with another blush, I stepped aside.

However, instead of mounting, he rubbed the back of his neck. "Ivy, will you be at the dance in two weeks?"

A dance? It was the first I knew anything about a dance. Was there a reason I hadn't been told about it? A dance sounded fun, and I couldn't think of any reason why I wouldn't go. Just because I couldn't hear the music didn't mean I couldn't dance. I gave a nod, and a grin appeared on his face.

"Good. That...good," he said as he adjusted his hat. He paused for another moment and then mounted the horse. He tipped his hat towards me and said something to Simon.

I stepped back as he kicked the horse into action and I watched him ride in the direction of the house and barns. Simon came up beside me. There was a grin on his face, which I chose to ignore.

My brother nudged my shoulder until I finally looked at him. "We should get back, too," was all he said.

As much I as I didn't want to return, I knew we'd been gone long enough. We started walking back. To my surprise, Simon put his arm around me.

Right at that moment, I was the happiest I'd been in months.

Chapter Fourteen

It was the Sunday after my conversation with Simon that I realized something important, and once I saw it, I was amazed that I hadn't noticed it sooner. The day seemed hotter than usual, and no breeze blew to counteract the sun's rays. Once I was finished eating, I leaned back on the blanket my family had spread and watched everyone. After all, what other entertainment did I have?

Watching the other people moving from blanket to blanket, and the children running and playing together was fun. It wasn't hard to see who were close friends, and who preferred to remain a little standoffish.

Before long, I noticed that Father had walked away to have a private conversation and my step-mother stood alone.

When I'd gone to my aunt's congregation in Springfield, there had been women who were expecting. Every Sunday, the women had flocked around those expectant mothers to chatter about the coming child and the preparations that had been done. With my step-mother's belly growing so big, I expected to see the same thing happen.

But I didn't.

Besides the reverend's wife, who had spoken to my family before the meal began, no one approached Cordelia. I saw many glances in her direction, but that was as far as it went. When I thought back to the few Sundays where I had attended church, I couldn't think of a single instance where someone had approached my step-mother. Yes, I had seen many speaking to Father, and Cordelia had been by his side each time. I assumed she'd participated in the conversation, but after seeing her isolation, doubt crept in.

As I watched, Father gestured for his wife to join him, and he addressed some statement to her. Her back was to me, so I couldn't see what she said. However, I could see the reaction of our neighbor. He gave a nod, acknowledging whatever it was Cordelia said and then turned his gaze back to Father. A moment later, he moved on his way.

Why didn't anyone carry on a conversation with her?

I couldn't hide my curiosity, but I was sure no one would realize what I was curious about. There wasn't a discreet way to ask Simon or anyone else, so I resolved to wait until later to find out what I could. Maybe her isolation was the reason for how she treated me. I knew all too well how awful it was to feel completely alone.

To distract myself, I turned my attention back to watching everyone else. I saw Anna with her friends near the pond. Someone sat beside me, but I assumed it was Simon. A hand touched my knee. Startled, I twisted around and found John Dover was the one who had taken a seat on the blanket next to me.

The grin on his face unsettled me. I shoved his hand away. How could I make it clear that I had no desire for his attention?

"Go away," I said, pointing.

He flinched, so I may have spoken a little louder than was necessary. Mr. Dover didn't make any move to leave though. Instead, he again reached his hand towards me. I slapped it away, glaring at him.

"Now, Miss Steele," he said, his smile becoming strained.

Why was he so close to me? I shifted away, wishing one of my family would notice and come to my rescue. Did no one see? When I'd been observing them, everyone had been going about their business and conversation. What would it take for someone to come to my aid?

A shadow fell over me, and I lifted my gaze. It was Remy, looking handsome cleaned up. He crouched down to be at my level. "Would you walk with me?" he asked, speaking in that considerately slow manner.

Relieved, I gave a nod and scrambled up. Remy straightened up and held out his hand to help me. I expected him to pull his hand away from me as soon as I was on my feet, but he didn't. He shifted his gaze to Mr. Dover, who was scowling. "Dover," I saw Remy say.

"Prater," Mr. Dover said in answer.

Tugging on my hand, Remy walked away, and I followed. We had only gone a few steps when Anna was suddenly in front of us. "There you are, Will," I watched her say. Right. Others called him by his first name. Though there was a smile on her face, Anna's eyes held an intense fury when she glanced at me. "Mary and...."

She brought her hand up to her mouth as she spoke and I lost what she said. Confused, I glanced at my escort. There was a frown on his face, and he shook his head. With his right hand, he brought my stepsister's hand down. "Not now, Miss Conway."

Oh, that was something else I hadn't known. Anna's last name was Conway.

"You will dance with me at the Smithsons' dance." I couldn't tell if Anna was asking a question or trying to make a statement with those words. Curious to know what Remy's answer would be, I swung my gaze to him.

"We will see."

He stepped to the side and, keeping a firm grip on my hand, went around Anna. I couldn't resist glancing over my shoulder at her. There could be no mistaking her fury as she twisted to watch us.

Though it hadn't been my intention, I'd just given her more reason to hate me.

IT DIDN'T TAKE ANNA long to make clear just how angry she was with me. As soon as the wagon pulled to a stop in front of the house, she pushed me to get off first. Then, when I jumped to the ground and started for the porch, she stuck her foot in front of me and tripped me.

She was careful, of course, not to do it so that others could see her. I managed to keep from hitting the ground, and my step-sister sailed past me as though nothing were wrong. I glared at her back.

If this was the way she wanted it, then I would just have to be satisfied knowing she'd started it.

Fighting over a person was the height of stupidity to me. It wasn't right; I didn't own Remy or his affections. A terrible war had been fought to make ownership of a person illegal. Oh, I knew there were other aspects of the war, but that was beside the point.

Approaching me, holding my hand, and walking with me in broad view of everyone in the congregation had been a bold move on Remy's part. A man didn't do something like that unless he was interested in a girl.

If Remy was interested in me—and my heart did a slight flutter as I thought about it—then that was his choice to make, whether anyone else approved or not. I wasn't adverse to a courtship between us. He was a hardworking, kind man. Only a fool would turn down such a man's attention.

Anna would just have to find a way to accept that.

She kept her distance until it came time for evening chores. Then, she made her displeasure known once again. I had yet to get the hang of milking the cow, and Anna had handled that chore, being too impatient to help me learn better.

That night, however, she shoved the bucket into my hands. "Learn to be useful," she said, her face so close to mine that I could smell her breath. Before I could pull away, she spun around and stalked toward the chicken coop.

She expected me to fail; I did not doubt that. Well, I wasn't about to prove her right.

I entered the barn, determined to do my task and return to the house as soon as possible. In the time I'd been on the ranch, I'd learned the basics of milking a cow. Somehow—I wasn't sure exactly how—I would make it work.

Everything was going fine until Anna entered the barn. I saw her come up beside me. All the sudden, the cow lurched forward and kicked the bucket. Though I tripped to catch it, the milk I'd managed to get from animal splashed to the ground as the bucket tipped over.

The milk soaked into the straw as I helplessly watched. I lifted my head as Anna walked past. There was a malicious smile on her lips. She'd done something, made some noise she knew I wouldn't be aware of, to startle the cow. Swiftly, I grabbed her wrist and pulled her to a halt.

For a moment, we just glared at each other.

"Why?" I signed with my right hand as I mouthed the word.

"Did I do something?" she said, not even pretending to misunderstand me. "Did you see me do something? Who will you tell?"

Frustrated, I shoved her hand away and let her go. There was still some milk left in the bucket, and I hadn't finished milking the cow. Cordelia would just have to be satisfied with a smaller amount.

If Anna expected me to come down any more to her level, she was wrong. I would turn the other cheek. Sooner or later, Father or Simon, maybe even Remy, would see her behavior and she would regret it.

With that decided, I just had to endure whatever she threw at me.

It couldn't be as bad as what Uncle Richard had put me through.

AS EXPECTED, CORDELIA was furious about how little milk there was. There was nothing I could do other than to mime that the bucket had fallen over. She rolled her eyes and spun around to continue cooking. As I watched, her head turned towards her daughter, who made sure to keep her back to me.

I had no doubt my step-sister was relaying some embellished story of how I had failed, and I braced myself for a scolding from Father after dinner. What I didn't expect was for Cordelia to meet Father's eyes as soon as the meal was over.

With a sigh, Father went to retrieve paper from the desk. Cordelia shooed everyone away from the table, leaving just Father and I. Apprehensive, I watched him write and mentally formulated my defense.

John Dover has asked to marry you.

Astonished, I stared at the words. John Dover? Marry? After I had repeatedly shunned him? What kind of fool was he? I didn't even need a minute to consider it and shook my head.

Father sent a look towards the kitchen before he began to write again. Was Cordelia encouraging this? I pursed my lips and waited to see what else my father had to say on the matter. Not that anything was going to change my mind.

He is a good man. His father is a successful businessman. He will be able to provide for you. You will not get a better offer than this.

Because I was deaf? Somehow I could not believe that in a territory where the men certainly outnumbered the women that such would be the case. John Dover, a man who I hadn't seen anything to like, couldn't be the only man to show an interest in me.

Since the shake of my head hadn't been enough before, I grasped the pen and scribbled my answer underneath his words. *No.*

Which was apparently not what my father expected. His eyebrows raised, he stared at me. After a moment, his gaze shifted once again to the kitchen, and I twisted around to see whom he was looking. Cordelia was facing us, and her arms were crossed. Did she guess that I was not cooperating?

"I will not marry him," I said aloud and signed since I wanted it to be obvious where I stood on the issue. "You cannot make me."

I saw Simon sit up straighter in his seat by the fireplace. My brother stood up and came around the table. Before anyone could stop him, Simon grabbed the paper Father had been using to tell me about John Dover. As he read the words, my brother's expression hardened.

"No." One hand made the corresponding sign, though I couldn't tell whether that was a conscious decision. He used his other hand to crumble the paper into a ball, even though it still had plenty of space for other writing. "Why would you even encourage this?"

Our stepmother hurried over. "Mr. Dover's offer is...."

"I wouldn't give him a dog I hated, let alone my only sister," Simon said with slow deliberation.

If that didn't set the fox among the hens, I didn't know what would.

"This has nothing to do...you!" Cordelia's face was flushed red. "She cannot expect a home here for the rest of her life."

"You don't want a slave? You could have fooled me."

I couldn't tell which statement to focus on: Cordelia's desire for me to be out of her house or the fact that Simon had noticed what I was enduring. Cordelia's face lost all color, and she took a step back. With my hand on the table, I felt it jolt when my father brought his fist down on the oak, and I swung my gaze to him.

"Enough," he said, with a scowl. "Simon, apologize to Cordelia and your other sisters."

"When they apologize to Ivy," Simon said, his expression stubborn. "They have treated her like she is nothing since the moment she got here."

At first, I couldn't bring myself to be sorry the whole situation had begun since it was heart-warming to see my brother defending me. Then, I saw Katie cowering in the doorway, her eyes wide with fear. How loud were everyone else's voices that they were frightening her so?

Quickly, I pushed myself from my chair and made a bee-line toward the girl. "Sorry," I signed as I knelt in front of her. She launched herself at me and wrapped her arms around my neck. I stood up with her in my arms.

When I turned, Anna was right there, and she tried to pull Katie from me. The little girl tightened her grip on me, refusing to be dislodged. "Give her to me," my step-sister said, her face close to mine.

At the table, Father was pinching the bridge of his nose. Simon and Cordelia were facing each other, make broad gestures though I couldn't figure out what they were saying. Neither of them was backing down.

What was wrong with our family?

I had no doubt life hadn't been like this for them before I arrived. Whether Simon had liked Cordelia or not, he must have at least treated her with respect. I'd caused this and I had no way of making it better.

"...send her back to school if you didn't want her here!" I saw Simon yell. "She wanted...!"

Anna was still trying to take Katie from me and untangled the girl's arms from around my neck. I allowed my half-sister to be pulled away by Anna and bolted out of the house.

Let them argue without me.

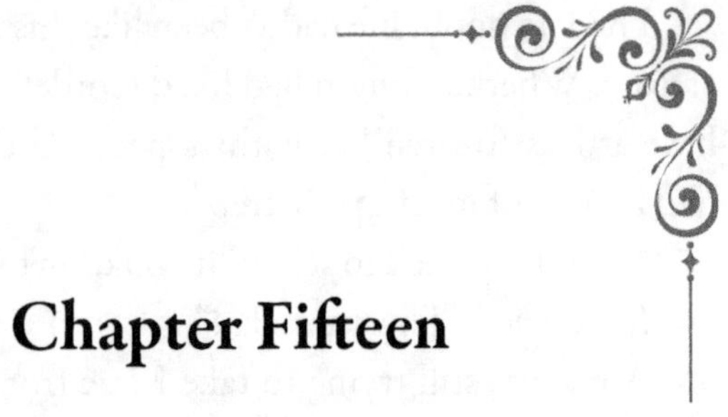

Chapter Fifteen

I t was dark out, but I didn't care as I plunged across the yard. The conflict in my family was too much for me to handle. What was so wrong with standing up for myself? Why was I not allowed to express an opinion in my own family?

School had taught me that I had worth, that I had importance as a person. Since rejoining my father and brother, I'd been forced to question that belief. I'd done few things right, and it had taken so long to reconnect with Simon that I'd begun to believe that I had no family I could rely on.

With tears blurring my vision, I stumbled my way through the dark. By memory, I made it to the corral. The horses shied as I collapsed against the fence. I took several deep breaths to calm myself.

I would never have thought I was one to run from my problems, but I seemed to be doing it quite a bit since coming to Montana. Though I suppose hiding from Uncle Richard had been a form of running.

Had I been running all my life?

Well, I wasn't going to keep doing it. With the back of my hand, I rubbed my eyes as I watched the horses pace in the corral. Tired. That's what I was: tired of always fighting to be treated as equal, as someone who was intelligent.

To my left there was movement, and I swung that way. Though his face was shadowed, I recognized my brother. He leaned against the fence, his arms folded on the top rail.

Matters must not have improved after I left.

Maybe he said something, but I couldn't see well enough to be sure.

The night grew darker and darker the longer we stood there. It was nice to know he had no desire to go back inside as well. Every time I glanced back, the windows remained aglow with light, so someone was still awake.

It was impossible to tell just how long we watched the horses pace the corral. I shivered as the night air continued to cool and I straightened up. There would be chores in the morning. Sulking outside in the dark and cold all night would only leave me tired, and in the end, what good would that do?

Reaching out, I put my hand on Simon's shoulder and squeezed gently to get his attention. When he glanced at me, I jerked my head towards the house. He shook his head. Hoping he would come inside later, I turned and walked back.

Only Father was in view when I stepped inside. He had his account book open, and he lifted his head as I closed the door. There were lines on his face that I hadn't noticed. I suppose worrying about whether your family was getting along would get stressful and leave its mark after a short time.

"Where is Simon?" was all he asked.

Since I didn't know whether my brother had moved from the corral or not, I gestured towards the outside in as vague a manner as I could. Father's frown deepened, and he shook his head. Without another word, he returned his focus to his figures. He brought his hand up to rub the side of his head.

Feeling dismissed, I went to the ladder and climbed up to the attic. Both of my step-sisters were awake, and I could see them whispering to each other as I went to my bed. I began to undress, and the candle on their side of the space went out, plunging the attic space into darkness.

I should have guessed.

SIMON DIDN'T COME TO breakfast in the morning. In fact, Anna didn't even set a place for him. How would she have known he wasn't coming? Had my brother said something? Never before had I felt I missed so much because of being deaf.

Father saddled his horse and rode away from the ranch alone. Would Simon meet him in town to work in the general store, or would Father have to handle everything on his own?

Cordelia refused to look in my direction. While Anna and Susan cleared the table and began washing the dishes, my step-mother went to the desk. She began to write, and I had a sinking feeling that whatever she was putting down on the paper was meant for me.

To put it off as much as I could, I went out to get the wash tub ready for the day's washing. Over at the corral, I could see Remy working with one of the horses. Fascinated, I paused and watched him brushing the horse's neck.

He always looked at home when he was with animals, and I'd never seen him have a problem with any four-legged creature. I wondered if he'd always had that skill, or if it was something that could be learned. Was he at ease with people as well? There'd been only a few occasions when I'd seen him around people other than my family, so I had no idea whether he was or not.

My skirt suddenly felt weighed down and then heat met my skin. Alarmed, I spun around and tried to pull the wet fabric away from my body. Anna dumped a bucket of steaming water into the tub. She'd tossed hot water at me on purpose!

"Enough," I said and signed at the same time. Couldn't she see there was enough trouble in the family without her antagonizing me? What did she hope to gain from me?

"If you don't want to be here, then leave," she said, for the first time speaking slow enough I could follow what she was saying.

Leave? Where did she expect me to go? She twisted around but then didn't go anywhere. I followed her gaze to see Cordelia at the kitchen door. My step-mother gestured for me to come to her. To do otherwise would have been disrespectful, so I walked over.

She held out a sheet of paper. Though I didn't want to, I took it from her. Cordelia turned and walked back into the kitchen, leaving me to read her message.

As your mother is not here to advise you, Ivy, I feel it falls on me to do so in her place. I do not think you have considered your future as a young woman in your position must.

How long do you expect to remain dependent on your father? He has four other children to provide for. Do you think that you can rely on your poor brother? Simon has his future to consider, and having his sister clinging to his sleeve will only hold him back from the man he should become.

My breath caught in my throat as my eyes moved over those words. How could she say such things? I was well aware of my father's responsibilities to his other children, my half-siblings. Even though I was deaf, I wasn't stupid. Never had I even thought Father should be focused exclusively on me.

And as to Simon, when had I ever *"clung to his sleeve"*?

Breathing out, I tried to steady my emotions as I read on.

Now, I'm sure if you took the time to know Mr. John Dover, you would realize as I do that he is an excellent match for any young lady, especially one in your situation. You must understand that you are at a severe disadvantage when it comes to having a secure future. Mr. Dover can give you that.

The paper shook so much in my hands that for a few seconds I couldn't continue reading. How dare she try to guilt me into accepting Mr. Dover's marriage proposal, one that he hadn't even made to me!

Anna went past me, her shoulder slamming into mine. I stumbled forward a step before I recovered my balance. As she continued walking, I glared at her back. There were just too many things for me to handle.

A shadow fell over me, and I twisted around to see Simon at my side. His facial expression was grim, and he took the paper from my hand. His mouth pressed into a thin line as he read what Cordelia had written.

I took the time to study my brother's face. Wherever he'd slept the previous night, he must not have gotten much rest. There were dark circles under his eyes, and his chin had the beginning of a beard.

By the time he was done reading, or maybe he didn't even finish, he crumpled the paper in his fist. He brought his other hand up and pinched the bridge of his nose, precisely as Father had the evening before.

"No," he said. "This cannot—will not—continue."

Though I was curious which situation he was referring to, I was a little afraid to ask. The last thing I wanted was to have a repeat of the previous evening. Nothing would be fixed, and the chasm that had developed in the family would only grow wider.

Or was inaction only going to make things worse?

With his free hand, Simon squeezed my shoulder and then moved forward. He dropped the balled-up paper and marched into the house. Kneeling down, I picked up my step-mother's message to me and began to smooth it out.

Once again, someone came up beside me, and I glanced over to see Remy. The cowboy wore a puzzled expression, his brow furrowed beneath his hat. "Something wrong?" he asked, facing me.

There was, but how could I explain it? I lowered my gaze to the paper in my hand. Cordelia had obviously meant the words only for me, but Simon had read it already. What was one more person? Especially one who lived on the ranch with the rest of us.

I held the paper out to him. His frown deepened as he took the paper from me. The muscles in his jaw tightened as his eyes moved across the page. For a moment, I thought he was going to do the same thing Simon had done and ball up the paper. Instead, he took a deep breath and handed it back to me.

At least now he knew what was wrong in my family.

The young man stayed beside me until Simon came out of the house. My brother had a carpet bag in one hand, and his expression was one of determination. Cordelia followed him out, coming to an abrupt halt as she saw Remy.

"Simon, don't...this," she said. "Wait for...father."

Since he had a bag of his belongings, I guessed he was leaving. What did he plan to do? Where would he go? How had it come to this?

Simon came to me, and his gaze moved from me to Remy. "Watch out for her," he said, while his eyes were on the cowboy. With one arm, he pulled me into a quick hug. With my ear next to his chest, I could feel the beat of his heart.

Too soon, he pulled away and stepped around me. I twisted around to watch him walk to his horse. He hooked the handles of his bag on the saddlehorn, and then he mounted. He didn't say anything else, as far as I could see, and just rode away.

When I turned back around, my stepmother's face was pale. Her gaze met mine, and her eyes narrowed into an accusing glare. She spun and vanished into the house. No doubt to document one other way I had wrought disaster on my family.

Feeling shaken and slightly guilty, I couldn't bring myself to look at Remy again. At that moment, Anna brought out the first basket of clothes. She sent a smile in the cowboy's direction as she set the basket down by the washtub.

If he hadn't been in sight, I think she would have dumped it on the ground.

Remy walked toward the corral. No matter what, there were still chores to be done by us all. Sighing, I went to the washtub and knelt down to begin the wash.

I DON'T THINK I'LL ever forget the look in my father's eyes when he returned home that night. Disbelief, despair, astonishment—all those emotions crossed his face in a matter of moments. Then he glanced at me.

Bracing myself, I held my breath and waited for him to blame me as Cordelia and Anna had already done.

All Father did was shake his head. Just as there had been for Simon, there were dark circles under my father's eyes. I could see the lines around his eyes and the years of his life showed more than they ever had before.

No one, besides Katie, spoke much at supper. The little girl seemed to have forgotten all about the tension and argument she'd witnessed the day before. Oh, to have the innocence of youth.

For the next three days, there was no sign of Simon. I did notice that Remy kept near the yard every day when the previous weeks he had been tending to fences and other tasks far from the house. If she hadn't joined Father in town to help at the store, I think Anna's animosity would have intensified.

Perhaps I had a poor opinion of my step-sister, but it was justified given everything she'd done and said to me since I'd arrived.

Cordelia spent more time in her rocking chair, mending baby clothes. Susan was put in charge of watching over Katie and young Sam, which left me to handle the daily chores that came with each day. To be honest, it was easier to keep busy. It kept me from worrying and overthinking.

On Thursday, Remy approached me while I was weeding the garden. When I lifted my gaze, I realized he had his hat in his hands and was shifting from side to side. What was he nervous about?

To my delight, he made the sign for my name and then he paused. Curious, I waited for him to say something. After a few seconds, he took a deep breath. "Do you dance?" he asked.

Did I dance? What an odd question! For a moment, I considered my answer with care. Even though we couldn't hear the music, my fellow students and I had danced several times over the years. Dances such as the Virginia Reel were fun with specific steps and movements that meant I didn't need the music once it began.

Remy's fingers had tightened on his hat. My hesitation was making him even more nervous. Taking pity on him, I gave a nod, and I watched as relief spread across his face.

"Will you go to the dance tomorrow night? With me?"

My breath caught in my throat. No one had ever asked me to attend a dance with them. Before, he'd asked if I was going to be there, but I hadn't imagined he would single me out like this.

After the way he'd held my hand after church when he rescued me from Mr. Dover's unwanted attention, there could be no doubt in my mind that he was interested in me. Even though I was deaf and my family didn't like me, he thought I might be worthy of being his life companion.

I gave a nod, and a grin appeared as he put his hat back on. "Good. I'm glad," he said. His gaze shifted toward the house. I glanced over and saw Cordelia waving her hand at us.

As Remy walked to join her, I turned my attention to the rows of beans in front of me. I couldn't keep the smile from my lips as I continued with my chore.

No one would ever be interested in a deaf girl who couldn't communicate in a way one could understand? I wondered how Cordelia would react when she realized that she was dead wrong.

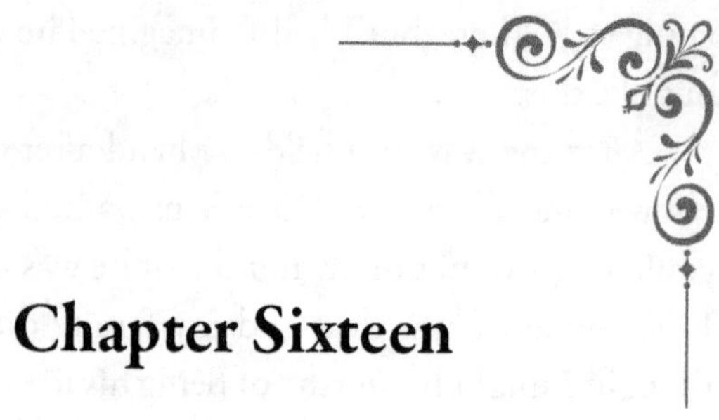

Chapter Sixteen

Of course, I had no idea how I was supposed to get to the dance with Remy. He surely wouldn't expect me to ride on his horse, would he? The thought was entertaining, at least.

At dinner that night, I asked Father if they were all going to the dance. Maybe Remy and I could ride to wherever the dance was being held with them? However, I followed Father's gaze, which he directed at Cordelia, and saw that the woman's fingers were clenching her fork so tight they were white. Would I ever get to the bottom of why everything seemed to offend my step-mother?

"We won't go," was all Father said to me.

Across from me, Anna scowled down at her plate. What was keeping them from attending? Was it because no one would speak to Cordelia, or was it because of me? How would they react when they learned I had been invited to go? Would they try to stop me?

Father's gaze went to the far end of the table where Remy was sitting. His eyes widening, Father stared at the cowboy. I could only guess that the cowboy had said something along the lines of that he was taking me to the dance, something I suppose was the respectful and correct course of action if he intended to start courting me.

Was I reading too much into his invitation to join him? Oh, I hoped not!

"What?" I saw Cordelia say. "Is this a joke?"

Why was I not surprised that was her first reaction? Heaven forbid anyone genuinely be interested in spending time with me.

"No, ma'am," Remy said. I could only guess that he was respectful because I couldn't imagine him being anything but polite.

When he said nothing else, I turned my attention to the rest of my family. Susan was ignoring everything in favor of cleaning off her plate. Sam was playing with his mashed potatoes, something Cordelia would have scolded him for if my step-mother had taken notice. Katie took advantage of the fact that Anna was staring at me in astonishment, and stole a piece of bread from Anna's plate.

Father's expression was one of confusion, and a frown creased his forehead. "You want to take Ivy to the dance?" And then he asked the question that I'd wondered about myself, but seemed offensive seeing someone else say it, "Why?"

A slight smile curved Remy's lips when I turned his way. "Because I know what it's like to be on the outside," he said with his usual deliberate slowness so that I would understand him.

How did he know? Every time I'd seen him with people, no one had treated him as if he were a pariah. Although, I had seen him keep his distance. What had happened to make him wary of others?

The table gave a jolt as Anna used it to shove her chair away. "What has happened to this family?" she asked. "This....all insane."

She stomped away and vanished up into the attic. My step-sister was taking the news as badly as I had expected. What new ways of torture would she come up with to punish me for this? Or would she finally give up making my life miserable since it wasn't exactly working out for her?

Time would tell, so I put it from my mind as I focused on Father once again. His expression was concerned but also...pleased? "I can see no reason why you shouldn't take Ivy," he finally said, causing Cordelia to swing her head towards him. "If she wants to go."

I don't think I would have been able to keep the smile from my face if lives had depended on it.

"....hear the music!" I only caught the last bit of Cordelia's sentence since she'd been facing away from me when she began speaking. "What is the point?"

Little did she know, I wouldn't need the music.

I SHOULDN'T HAVE BEEN surprised that when I dreamed that night, I heard music. Not just any music, either. My dream contained my mother singing.

Mother had loved to sing. My earliest memories of her were of her singing while she worked. Her favorites had been *"Annie Lawry," "Shenandoah,"* and *"Lily Dale,"* though on Sundays she would sing hymns. Whatever she was doing, Mother managed to have a song to go along with the task.

It was one of the things I missed the most after I woke up without hearing. That and the cheerful sound of birds chirping and singing in the morning.

So, it was understandable that after the times when I dreamed of hearing, the following day would be a rough one. I'd learned to adapt to my life without hearing, but that didn't mean I had forgotten what it was like to hear. There were times when I missed it, especially whenever I would realize there were things I was never going to hear.

Such as Remy's voice.

I'd clung to my memories of my father's voice and Simon's, though I'm sure my brother's voice must have deepened with age. Still, it was something.

With Remy, though, I would never know what his voice was like. Was it deep or more of a tenor? Did he have an accent from growing up in the West? Could he sing or was he tone-deaf? I could ask, of course, but it wouldn't be the same.

Cordelia didn't seem to notice any change in my behavior. She made sure I remained busy from the moment breakfast ended until late afternoon. Perhaps she thought to keep me from preparing for the dance. However, she had underestimated my ability to adapt to my surroundings and make do with what I had.

Tepid water in the pitcher was all I had to clean the dirt from my skin as I had no time for an actual bath. From my small trunk, I drew a small bottle of perfume that had belonged to my mother. I breathed in the subtle scent of lily of the valley as I dabbed a little behind my ears and on my wrists.

There was one dress I'd had no opportunity to wear since I'd come to Montana. Fortunately, it had traveled well, and there were no wrinkles, even from being packed in the trunk for so long. The vibrant blue color was my favorite, and the last gown Aunt Ruth had made for me.

The smell of frying ham reached me as I dressed and I felt my stomach gurgle with hunger. What kind of food would be at the dance?

I unplaited my hair and brushed it out. If I'd had the time and space, I would have liked to curl my hair, but that just wouldn't be possible. Smoothing my hair back, I separated my hair into two sections and braided each section. Using pins, I coiled both braids into a bun at the back of my neck.

Holding up my hand mirror, I admired myself for only a moment. My Sunday boots went on my feet and my only pair of lace gloves on my hands. I lifted my best hat from its little box but decided it wasn't necessary.

Just in case the night grew cold, I draped my wool shawl over my arm and climbed downstairs. Immediately, Katie came running to me. She ran her hands, thankfully clean, over my dress. Curious, Sam crawled over to see what fascinated her so.

Father had returned from town, and he walked to me. He took my hands in his. For a moment, his eyes glistened with tears. "You are the image of your mother," he said. Bending forward, he kissed my cheek.

My vision blurred with tears at his display of affection, but I managed a smile as he stepped back. I brought my hand up to my mouth and moved it away. "Thank you," I signed.

I didn't see Anna or Cordelia when I glanced around the room, and I wondered where they'd gone. Father's head turned towards the doorway, and when I glanced that way, I saw Remy standing there. My breath caught in my throat.

He was dressed in the same clothes he'd worn to church the previous week: a red, clean shirt and tan trousers. His boots shone in the light, and his hat seemed free of any dust or dirt. Remy looked exactly as I would imagine a handsome cowboy from the West would.

Hastily, as though he realized he'd been staring at me, he removed his hat. "Mr. Steele," he said, with a nod toward my father. He held his hand out to me. "Shall we go?"

Eager to be off, I walked to him, slipping my gloved hand into his bare one. Father stepped closer and stopped me from continuing by putting his hand on my shoulder. "Be back before midnight," he said, his expression serious.

"Yes sir," Remy said in answer.

His lips pursed, Father let go of me, and Remy led me outside. The wagon was waiting only a few yards from the porch. My escort helped me up to the seat and moved around to climb up himself.

Glancing over, I lifted my hand in a wave. Father stood on the porch with Sam in his arms and Katie clinging to his leg. All three of them waved back as the wagon jolted into motion.

I WAS SO EXCITED ABOUT the evening away from the ranch, and I could barely keep myself from bouncing on the seat. Remy was occupied with handling the reins, but now and then, he would look over at me with a slight smile. Maybe I wasn't doing such a good job of controlling how I was feeling.

Wherever we were going, it took quite awhile to get there, and the sun was going down. Soon, though, I could see many lights ahead of us and guessed that was our destination. Before we reached it, Remy slowed the wagon.

"What's wrong?" I asked and signed at the same time.

"Wait," Remy said. In the fading light, I had to squint to see his mouth.

Puzzled, I glanced around at the darkening landscape. After several moments, I spotted a horse and rider coming toward us. It wasn't until he was right next to the wagon that I recognized my brother. "Simon!"

It had only been a few days, but it was good to see him. Simon leaned over and gave me a one-armed hug. He stayed next to the wagon as we began moving again. I wasn't sure where to look: at him, Remy, or where we were going.

No more than ten minutes later, we were at the ranch. It was one that was close to town, I thought, but I couldn't be sure. Other wagons arrived at the same time. Remy parked the wagon next to a row of other wagons and buggies. He jumped to the ground and hurried to help me down. I waited a few steps away while he and Simon made sure the horses were cared for.

Then, my hand on Remy's arm and Simon on my other side, we walked to the brightly lit barn. I breathed in the scents of freshly cut pine and cooked food. At one end, a few older men were tuning their instruments and laughing together. The center of the barn was filled with people, and I was relieved to see that my dress wasn't the fanciest one there in the building.

Simon left my side almost immediately and vanished into the crowd. For a moment, I wished I'd taken the opportunity to ask him what he was doing. However, on second thought, perhaps that was more a subject for a private moment.

With ease, Remy led me through the barn. I couldn't tell where he was taking me until we were in front of Sheriff Worth, who was speaking to the reverend and the reverend's wife, Mary. The woman turned to me with a smile, her brown eyes bright.

"Ivy," she said. "I am glad to see you."

Wishing I knew the reverend's last name so I could think of him as something other than "the reverend," I smiled at her. "Where is the rest of your family?" she asked, after glancing around the barn. A puzzled frown creased her forehead.

"Not here," I said and signed, pulling my hand away from Remy's arm so that I could use my hands.

"Anna didn't say you would be here."

Anna didn't say I was coming? When had she talked to the reverend's wife about whether our family would come to the dance or not?

Before I could think any more about it, I saw that everyone's heads, including Mary's, turned towards the far end of the barn. A man, whom I vaguely recognized as having conversed with my father a few times after church, had his arms raised as though he were calling for everyone's attention. I was too far away to read his lips, so I had no idea what was happening.

Confused, I shifted my attention to Remy, trusting he would let me know if it was important or not. When he realized, a smile flashed across his lips, and he said, "Food."

Oh, it was time to eat already? A twinge in my stomach reminded me that it had been several hours since I'd last eaten.

Everyone else began to move towards the tables lined up against one wall. I couldn't keep my gaze in one place as Remy guided me to join the line. There were bales of straw all around, and small children were using them as seats and playthings.

When I reached the first of the tables, I couldn't believe the variety set out. Several ladies were dishing out the food for each person as they passed through the line. My plate was piled high by the time I reached the end, and I had no idea whether I would be able to eat it all.

Perched on one of the straw bales, I balanced my plate on my knee. Remy sat next to me. This was undoubtedly a situation where a couple could talk and get to know each other. However, between my deafness and so many people around, I couldn't work out how we could manage to do the same.

Somehow, despite my attention being all over the place with so much to be seen, I cleaned my plate. Remy took my plate and left me feeling thoroughly stuffed. I noticed that the center of the barn began to clear and couples had begun to form two lines. A tug on my hand made me glance over at Remy. He inclined his head towards the lines and raised his eyebrows.

Without saying a word, he asked me to dance.

With a smile, and hoping it would be a dance I knew, I let him lead me out to join the others. Out of the corner of my eye, I saw that the young lady I ended up next to cast a startled glance in my direction.

Though I wanted to glance around and get a better idea of the barn itself, I forced myself to keep my eyes on Remy. I had to trust him to lead me through the dance, and if I lost track of him...well, it would be nothing short of a disaster.

My partner smiled at me, his head bobbing slightly. Was he keeping time with the music? I saw the young woman next to me start forward and at the same time, Remy stepped forward. Hastily, I did the same. As Remy bowed towards me, I made a polite, slight curtsey before quickly moving back.

There were several variations of the Virginia Reel, and I knew I would have to be on my toes to keep up with whatever this one threw at me. Remy stepped forward again, holding his hands out. I did the same, and once we clasped hands, we made a complete turn. We then returned to our original places.

Once again, we met each other and passed each other, our right shoulders brushing. Without turning, we went around each other back-to-back and stepped back to our places. Then, we did the same thing, only our left shoulders brushed.

Everyone began to clap and, hoping I was keeping the right time, I did the same. The couple at the head of the line, their hands joined, came bouncing down to the end of the line and then returned to where they had started. I leaned forward so I could watch as they linked right arms and turned around once and a half.

The lady and her partner wove their way down the line until they reach the foot of the lines. It was a relief to participate once again instead of clapping along with everyone else. The couple joined hands across and moved to the head of the set. They separated and turned outwards. The man walked toward the foot directly behind the men's line, followed by all the men in single file. At the same time, the ladies did the same thing on our side of the set.

When the couple reached the foot of the set, they stopped, joined both hands to form an arch. I saw how everyone ahead of Remy and I joined hands before they went under the arch. By the time it was all over, the couple who had begun was at the foot.

My cheeks ached from smiling as I went through the steps of the dance. It was the most fun I'd had in a long time, especially when Remy and I were at the head of the line. I had no way of knowing whether I was in time with the music, but it didn't seem to matter. Everyone appeared to be laughing and smiling.

After Remy and I made the arch, and the other couples moved under, the dance came to an end. Feeling out of breath but exuberant, I clapped my hands enthusiastically. While several pairs walked to the sidelines, others began to reform into new lines.

Reaching over, Remy caught my hand and gave a slight shake of his head. Although I wanted to dance more, he must have had his reasons for sitting out this dance. He led me towards the punch bowl, and as he ladled some of the liquid into glasses, I watched the dancers.

I couldn't recognize the pattern they were dancing, and when I glanced towards the musicians, I saw one of them call out. Perhaps that was why Remy had decided we wouldn't participate if it were a dance that relied on the dancers hearing what steps were being chosen on the spot.

With a sigh, I shook my head and let my gaze wander the rest of the barn. There were some I recognized, and others I didn't. Then, I saw a young woman with long, shiny black hair on the opposite side of the barn. Her head was tilted back in a laugh. Was that...Anna? What was she doing at the dance when Father said no one else in our family was attending?

Chapter Seventeen

Two gentlemen passed in front of me, and I lost sight of my step-sister. Confused, I tried to find her again. How had she gotten here from the ranch? Did Father know she'd come?

Questions filled my head, but I was quickly distracted. Someone's fingers curled around my arm and pulled me around. "Miss Steele," Mr. John Dover said, his face near mine. I could smell beer on his breath, and it turned my stomach. "Come dance."

Clearly, he didn't have the sensitivity that Remy did. I shook my head and tried to pull away. He only tightened his grip. "I insist," he said.

Remy shifted closer. However, he didn't say anything. It only took me a moment to realize what he was doing, and my respect for him just grew. He was allowing me to decide for myself, and merely being close to back me up on my choice.

"No thank you, sir," I said, signing the words out of habit.

A muscle in Mr. Dover's jaw twitched, and his eyes narrowed slightly. His dark hair was oily and smoothed back. "Miss Steele, I...not take no for...answer."

"I said no!" This time, I was certain my voice was louder than before. Men and women standing nearby all turned towards us. Blood rushed to my cheeks as I realized we were causing a scene. "Please let go of me."

This time, Remy stepped forward and wrapped his hand around Mr. Dover's wrist. My escort forced the man to let go of me and pushed him away. If he said anything, I didn't see it. All I knew that more people were staring at us.

Sheriff Worth was suddenly in between Remy and Mr. Dover, and Simon was at my side. Now there could be no doubt we were the center of attention. Even the couples dancing had come to a halt.

Mr. Dover held his hands up, a sneer on his face. Though I expected him to retaliate or say something, he spun on his heel and walked away.

I let out the breath I hadn't realized I was holding. The sheriff waved his hands, and everyone who had been watching the scene moved away. My embarrassment and dismay didn't lessen, though. Remy had brought me to the dance to have fun, and I didn't want to ruin that for him or anyone else.

Remy's fingers linked with mine and he gave a slight, reassuring squeeze. I forced a smile as I focused on him. A hand waving on my right made me turn toward my brother. "Are you all right?" he asked, concern in his eyes.

At the same time, the reverend's wife came toward us. Heavens, I would continue to be the center of attention if everyone kept asking me how I was.

"I am fine," I signed and said so there would be no doubt. All I wished was that everyone would put it behind them.

Yes, it happened, and because I hoped it wouldn't happen again, it wasn't something I could ignore completely.

With a slight smile, as though he understood my feelings, Remy handed me a glass of punch that he'd been holding onto since Mr. Dover had made a scene. With relief, I took one of the drinks and sipped the liquid, wrinkling my nose at the slightly woody taste beneath the fruit.

What was in the punch?

I watched as Remy took his first sip and his eyebrows went up. He sent a glance towards the reverend's wife and said something. The woman's eyes widened with what could only be horror, and she rushed away.

Beside me, Simon bent over in laughter, and I wondered what the joke was. Remy took my glass from my hand. He hurried away with it, which made me frown. I was still thirsty.

Recovering himself, Simon straightened himself and stepped closer. He put his arm around my shoulders and began to watch the dancers. Breathing out, I focused on everyone in the barn. There was bound to be enough to keep me well occupied until I could dance again.

MR. DOVER DISAPPEARED for the rest of the night, for which I was grateful, especially since Remy wasn't the only person I danced with. I expected Simon to ask me to dance, but he seemed to be interested in a red-haired young woman.

I had no idea what the time was when I needed to make my way to the outhouses. Simon and Remy were in conversation, and I could see no one I knew, so I decided to handle the matter on my own. The cold night air made me shiver when I stepped into the open, and I kept my steps quick as I crossed the distance between the barn and the outhouse.

The only light was the half moon in the sky and the stars that were more brilliant than I'd ever seen in Springfield or at school. Once I finished relieving myself, I took my time as I walked back so that I could enjoy the sight.

Though I'd seen it over a hundred times already since coming to the Montana territory, I doubted I would ever tire of the vast sky overhead.

Movement in the darkness caught my attention, and I came to a halt. A woman came rushing from the shadows to my left, and a man followed soon after. Though I couldn't make out who they were, I saw the woman glance over her shoulder and then slow her steps so the man caught up to her with ease.

My cheeks heated up with embarrassment. I'd seen several such scenes play out at school and I could guess what the couple had been doing in the dark. Then, the couple parted ways, with the woman hurrying to the door of the barn. As the lantern light fell on her face, I caught my breath.

Anna?

A second later, she vanished inside. Confused, I shook my head to clear my thoughts. How long had Anna been interested in someone who wasn't Remy? She'd been so jealous of him taking me to the dance earlier, but her familiarity with the man hinted that she must have known him well.

Should I tell my father? I didn't see how I could keep it to myself. If there was one thing I knew all too well, it was that a girl's reputation needed to be spotless. Would I be bringing down more trouble onto my family if I did speak?

Unnerved and uncertain what I should do, I hurried into the barn. I caught Remy's eye, and he rushed over. "Is something wrong?" he asked in concern.

I shook my head. Well, there was something wrong, but it was too difficult to explain. Remy glanced around the room before returning his gaze to me. "Do you want to leave?"

As much as I hated to cut short what had been the most enjoyable evening I'd ever had, I was too unsettled to put on an unconcerned front for much longer. It would take too much energy. I said, my hand making the brief sign, "Please."

With a nod, Remy escorted me to where my shawl was. Somehow, he managed to catch my brother's eye, and Simon came over. "Leaving already?" my brother asked, his eyebrows raised. "It's...early."

Confident Remy would explain, I took a moment to cast one last look at the scene. Everyone appeared happy, their eyes bright with laughter and their lips spread in wide grins. How long would it be before such an evening occurred again? Although I regretted taking my leave, I knew it would be for the best.

On my arm, Remy's fingers tightened ever so slightly, and I refocused on him. He inclined his head toward where our host and hostess were speaking with the sheriff. I nodded, and we began walking in that direction.

How easily Remy had learned to communicate with me in subtle ways that didn't make me feel inferior!

In a matter of minutes, Remy had thanked the couple for having us, and I'd managed to convey my pleasure at the evening. Then, it was out the door. Simon stood with me just outside the barn while Remy went to get the wagon. That was when my brother took the opportunity to press a folded slip of paper in my hand.

Surprised, I glanced at it before frowning at Simon. He was gazing out into the darkness, his lips pursed as though he were whistling. I slipped the letter, or message, into my handbag to read once I was home.

Five minutes later, Simon helped me into the wagon. When I glanced over my shoulder as the wagon set into motion, he was entering the barn, no doubt to find the redheaded girl again. As happy as I had been to see him, it still pulled at my heart that he was not at home, that he was estranged from Father because of me.

Though I tightened my shawl around my arms, the fresh air made me shiver. To my surprise, Remy shifted the reins into his left hand and put his right arm around me.

My breath caught in my throat. We'd waltzed earlier, and being so close to him as he swept around the dance floor, had been a novel experience. To put his arm around my shoulders was more of a comforting move, but so few people had ever had an interest in how I was feeling.

He must have heard me because he immediately pulled his arm away. With a huff, I caught his hand and pulled it back, shifting to be closer to his side.

I angled my head to glance at him and in the dim moonlight, I could see the broad smile on his face. My smile tugged at my lips as I focused on the horses pulling the wagon.

If I had to choose a perfect way to end a beautiful night, this would be it.

The drive home seemed short, and soon Remy was helping me to the ground in front of the house. By this time, it was too dark to see anything, but I saw him tip his hat to me. He waited until I was on the porch before he drove the wagon to the barn where he would put the horses away.

Though I wasn't ready to return to everyday life, I opened the front door and entered. Alone, Father was sitting in front of the fireplace, book in hand. The small fire provided the only light source, so it was difficult to believe he'd been reading. He glanced my way, closed the book in his hand. I saw him rise from his chair as I shut the door.

Honestly, I expected him to say something, but all he did was walk to his bedroom door and vanish from sight. Well. At least he'd waited to make sure I arrived home, which then begged one crucial question.

When and how was Anna going to come home?

IT WAS HARDER THAN I expected to drag myself out of bed come dawn. Susan, who would take any opportunity to stay in bed, was already dressed when I sat up. She rushed out of sight without a glance at me. As I dressed, I resigned myself to enduring my step-mother's wrath for being lazy. After the evening I'd had, though, it was worth it.

The scent of burning bacon reached my nose as I finished coiling my hair into a proper bun at the back of my neck.

Puzzled, because my step-mother had never burnt a thing as far as I knew, I climbed down the ladder and faced the kitchen. There was no sign of Cordelia, and it was Susan at the stove. A smoky haze filled the air.

Why wasn't my step-mother helping her? Susan may have been old enough to cook, but it was apparent she was still learning. My young step-sister also had chores to care for, and since I knew she'd just risen, she couldn't have done them yet.

Filled with confusion at the sudden break from normality, I hurried to the stove. Relief spread across Susan's face as I gently shifted her away from the hot surface. With ease, I removed the black pieces of meat from the frying pan and set the iron object away from the heat.

How had Susan managed to destroy breakfast in so short a time?

When I glanced over, the young adolescent had tears in her eyes, and I felt a twinge of guilt for my harsh thoughts.

"What's wrong?" I asked, unable to sign with a fork in one hand and a towel to keep from burning myself in my left.

She flinched, and her eyes flicked toward the closed bedroom door. When her gaze came back to me, she just shook her head. Head ducked down, she put the eggs on the table and escaped out the door with the empty egg basket.

With a sigh, I left the stove to mix up a batch of flapjacks to give the bacon fat time to cool down a little before I attempted to fry up more. There was a delicate balance needed whenever it came to preparing a meal. I wanted each item to be done properly and ready at the same time, so I had to plan out when to begin cooking.

I did not have time to think as I moved between the stove and the table. Every second, I expected Cordelia to come flying from her room, furious to see me in her kitchen. But the door remained firmly closed. This was my chance to prove I was capable of managing the kitchen.

Susan brought in fresh eggs and milk. She rushed to the second bedroom. Hoping she was getting Sam and Katie, I set the plate of flapjacks in the middle of the table. Movement near the door caught my attention, and when I glanced over, I saw Remy.

His eyebrows raised, he nodded towards me. His eyes moved quickly over the scene. To convey my ignorance of what was going on, I shrugged and focused on the food.

To my surprise, Remy came over and took the bowl of scrambled eggs from me when I finished filling it. He set it on the table and returned to my side. I handed him the plate of unburnt bacon, and he immediately picked up a piece. He grinned at my gasp of outrage and then put the plate on the table.

All that was left was...the coffee. I'd forgotten to start the coffee! Alarmed, I lunged for the coffee pot. Where did Cordelia keep the coffee beans? Did they need to be ground? How could I have forgotten Father always drank coffee at breakfast?

In my haste, the pot fell from my fingers, hit the edge of the stove, and landed on the floor. Old coffee splashed all over the wooden boards. Appalled, I grabbed the closest towel and knelt down to clean up the mess. Would it be now when Cordelia appeared, full of criticism and judgment for my error?

Remy knelt beside me. He straightened the metal coffee pot and nudged it towards me. With his other hand, he took the towel from me and began mopping up the old coffee.

Breathing out, I picked up the coffee pot and picked it up. As soon as I straightened, I realized Susan had brought out Sam and Katie. My half-siblings were laughing and pointing at the mess on the floor.

I felt my blood rush to my cheeks. Her expression one of amusement, Susan let go of Sam's hand and stepped forward. She went to the shelf over the stove and pulled a small bag down. Before she opened it, I could smell the coffee beans. Without a word, my younger step-sister held it out to me.

Relieved, I took the bag and hurried to make the coffee. There was no sign of Father yet, so I hoped I would get the hot drink finished before he came out.

Chapter Eighteen

Thankfully, since I'd covered each dish, breakfast was still warm when Father came out of the bedroom. The expression on his face was grave, and he said nothing as he filled a plate. He carried it to the bedroom and then returned. Once the rest of us were seated, with Father at the head of the table, the three vacant seats were obvious.

I kept my eyes moving throughout the meal. The only thing said was when Father would tell Katie to sit still and eat. Every couple of minutes, Remy would meet my gaze and send a slight smile at me. It was reassuring in an atmosphere that was full of tension.

The moment everyone was done, Father rose and left the house, no doubt to hitch up the horses. Susan, who'd kept Sam on her lap and made sure he ate, kept the two young ones occupied. I cleared the dishes and placed them in the sink.

Determined not to anger Cordelia, I set about washing them as quickly as possible. Remy once again surprised me by picking up a clean towel and drying the dishes as I rinsed the soap from them. In no time at all, the task was completed with all everything in its place.

As I hurried to the door, I sent a glance at the closed bedroom door. Was Cordelia feeling unwell? Her belly had grown so much in the last few weeks. It was only a matter of time before I would have a new half-sibling.

I'd kept my brother's letter in my pocket, waiting for the right moment to read it. I found that moment on the way into town for church. Father drove the wagon, and Susan kept Katie and Sam occupied in the back. Glancing over at my father to make sure his eyes were on the road, I unfolded the paper and began to read.

Ivy,

When I think of the past couple of months, I am ashamed at how long I've let Cordelia take advantage of your presence. She has been unfair, and her actions are a judgment on her.

Of course, I am not entirely blameless. There is no excuse for how I have behaved since you joined us. No doubt Cordelia believed no one would stand up for you, and I should have long before this point. I don't deserve it, but will you forgive me for being selfish and uncaring when I should have been the one person you could rely on?

The point of this message is not merely to apologize to you but to tell you that I am working on a way to provide a place for you and me, far from Cordelia. Although I hate to abandon Father, he has made his choice, and I've decided it is time to make mine.

If you can endure Cordelia and Anna a little longer, I will get everything in order so that you and I can strike out on our own.

Simon

Breathing out, I lifted my gaze to where Remy was riding ahead of the wagon. Did he know about my brother's proposal? I would have to ask him.

The wagon jolted as it hit a pothole and I grabbed the edge of the seat to keep my balance. Father was, in general, careful when driving, making sure to avoid such occurrences. A glance showed that he was staring straight ahead with a worried frown on his face.

If I were to leave the ranch for wherever Simon found a place for us, what would it do to Father? Would he be relieved to see me gone, or would he be saddened as he had been when Simon rode away? To set up a home with just my brother had a ring of finality about it.

For me, it would be a relief to escape the judgment and unkindness of Cordelia and Anna.

Carefully, I refolded the letter and slipped it away. Such a decision could not be made on a whim. I would consider it, weigh the pros and cons as Aunt Ruth had taught me to do.

Aunt Ruth. It had been several weeks since I'd last thought of my poor aunt. Guilt made me close my eyes. Was it selfish to put what had happened behind me? Even the happy memories, few though they had been, still seemed tainted by her sudden death.

Feeling the wagon slow, I opened my eyes to see the edge of town. Time had flown by with my introspection.

Maybe time in God's house would provide me with some peace of mind.

ANNA WAS PRESENT AT the church, dressed in the same dark blue dress I'd seen her wearing the evening before at the dance. I first saw her laughing with her friends, whom I had yet to meet. Then, when the service began, she didn't sit with us but was closer to the pulpit.

It would have been impossible not to observe my brother slip in right as everyone rose for the first hymn. He sat on the edge of the pew in front of me. I saw Father glance at Simon.

Maybe there was a chance they would resolve their differences. I had the feeling there was more to it than just how I had been treated.

As soon as the final amen was uttered, however, Father ushered us all out the door, not stopping to speak to anyone. He sent Susan to get Anna and then lifted the two little ones into the back of the wagon.

A hand on my shoulder made me start, and I spun around to find myself inches from Mr. John Dover. What would it take to convince the man that I had no interest in him? Why did he keep persisting in his pursuit?

The man offered a slight bow and held out a bouquet of wildflowers. There was a smile on his face but his eyes....his eyes held hatred. If he disliked me, why did he continue to approach me? Was he simply angry that I had refused him?

In any event, there was no way I was taking those flowers from him. He'd no doubt take it as a sign that I was softening towards him. Then he would be even more annoying than ever. I shook my head and took a step back. The side of the wagon pressed against my back, and the feeling of being trapped intensified.

Simon and Remy were nowhere in sight when I glanced around. In fact, where had Father gone? Well, I'd had plenty of opportunities to stand up for myself, although knowing I had someone on my side to intervene if necessary would have been a comfort.

"I have no interest in you," I said and signed, my hands moving quickly. Maybe this would be enough to make him take his attention elsewhere. "Please leave me alone."

Mr. Dover's eyes narrowed as they watched my hands. A muscle twitched in his jaw. He didn't like to see me sign. I hadn't stopped for Anna, and I wasn't about to change for him. Raising my chin, I stared at him.

"You are...stupid girl," he said, his lip curling up in disgust. He threw the bouquet at my feet "I...willing to take you. Who else will? No one with...sense."

If he was so angry with me that he would insult me, why did he bother to approach me with flowers? Had he been put up to it? Anna had taken such an interest in the matter, and I wouldn't have been surprised if she had a part in this current confrontation. It was difficult to tell who wished me gone more, her or her mother.

"You...even understand."

Had I missed a word? He spoke rather quickly at times. Did he mean I didn't understand? Because I did understand. He thought he was doing me a favor in bestowing his attention on me. Little did *he* understand that I didn't need or want him.

"You are a stupid girl," Mr. Dover said again. When I tried to step to the side to get away from him, he made a corresponding step and blocked me. "What good are you?"

Was he going to stand there and insult me? Just when I thought I would have to resort to violence—a kick to the ankle, perhaps—to get away from him, out of the corner of my eye, I saw Father come around the horses. "Papa," left my lips before I even thought about it. I hadn't called him that since I was Katie's age.

Father came to a halt and looked between Mr. Dover and me. For a moment, I held my breath, waiting to see what his reaction would be. Would he believe, like Cordelia, that I should accept Mr. Dover's attention, or would he see how much I did not want to be where I was?

"Come, Ivy," Father said, gesturing for me. "We...going home. John."

Mr. Dover took a step back and spun away. Over his shoulder, I could see Anna staring at the scene with a frustrated expression. She put on a smile as she approached, and climbed onto the wagon bench.

One thing was clear: my step-sister and I would have to have a discussion and make a few things clear between us.

THE DOWNSTAIRS BEDROOM door was still closed when we entered, and Father went in. Anna immediately rushed to the kitchen and began to pull out food for a makeshift midday meal. Since I had made breakfast, I was more than happy to let her take charge now.

Katie tugged on my hand to get my attention and showed me the doll I'd given her. Somehow, she'd managed to tear the dress. My half-sister's eyes glittered with tears. Kneeling down, I mimed sewing with a needle and thread, promising to repair the damage. Rubbing her face, she nod-ded.

Once the fried ham and potatoes were on the table, Father came out. "...mother...unwell," he said, focusing on Anna.

She nodded, her face devoid of any sympathy. After that, there was nothing else spoken at the table. The first chance she had, Susan vanished outside. Anna put Sam down for a nap, and Katie settled in front of the fireplace with a wooden object that had a vaguely human shape. Father opened up his account books.

It didn't take long to mend the tear in the doll's dress, and I made a mental note to sew a new one when I got my hands on some scrap pieces of fabric. Once I turned the toy back over to Katie's care, I decided to take advantage of the beautiful day to do some sketches outside. With my paper and pencils in hand, I left the house.

When I stepped off the porch, I saw a second shadow and realized I'd been followed. When I turned, I found my step-sister. Well, I'd wanted to have a conversation with her anyway.

"You are a fool." There was no mistaking what Anna said since she was inches from my face, and she made sure to speak in an exaggerated way.

"Why?" I asked. She was welcome to her own opinion, of course, but it would be nice to know the reason behind why she thought so little of me.

She threw up her hands and shook her head. "John Dover wanted you, and you said no."

Was that supposed to matter to me? I shrugged my shoulders to convey how little I cared about the man and his desires. My stepsister's face darkened, and she grabbed my sketchbook from my hand. "Hey!" I tried to grab it back, but she knelt down and used the step as a makeshift desk to write on.

Was it so difficult for her to ask if she could use my paper instead of just grabbing it?

Anna's expression was a mixture of defiance and victory when she handed the paper back.

There are times when a woman has few options and must take whatever she can get. You have even less. If you think Will Prater will marry you, you don't know his history as I do. John Dover at least was willing to take you even though you are inferior and so far beneath him.

My breath caught in my throat as I stared at the words. Inferior? He would take me? What part of those comments wasn't insulting? I didn't want someone who wanted me in spite of my deafness, but someone who accepted me as I was. Of course, I didn't know all that much about Remy's history. We hadn't had a chance to know each other well.

But what stood out to me the most was the first line: *a woman must take whatever she can get.* Shaken by the implications of those words, I lifted my gaze to her and asked, "Is that why your mother married my father?" I didn't care whether my voice was too loud and someone else would hear me.

Anna's face froze for just a moment and then she laughed. "What about it?"

My heart dropped. I was right, then. Cordelia had married my father for reasons that had nothing to do with loving him. Had she just wanted a home for her children and marriage was her only option? How had she gone about accomplishing it? Had she manipulated my father? After all, Anna must have learned it from someone.

Did Father know?

The smugness on Anna's face was too much for me to bear. I knew it was a bad idea, but the desire to hurt her as much as she'd hurt me was too much to resist. "Why do people hate your mother?"

She recoiled, her eyes widening. "Shut your mouth. You know nothing!"

There was something, then. Well, I would have to discover the truth when there wasn't something more important to make clear. To ensure that she would not misunderstand me, I wrote out my response to her.

I will not, nor will I ever, consent to marriage to a man who thinks of me as inferior. Do not think you will change my mind. I will not tolerate any further interference in my life, so do not encourage Mr. Dover. He made his real feelings clear enough today and ought to be wise enough to move on.

Nothing else needed to be said. I tore off the page, slapped it into her hand, and spun to be on my way. I'd only gone a few steps before I remembered there was one more thing I wanted to know. When I twisted around, Anna had balled up the paper and thrown it on the ground.

"We should have your beau to dinner sometime soon," I said, not even bothering to sign the words. "After all, you and he must be serious if you're sneaking off into the shadows for some time alone."

All color drained from Anna's face, and she staggered back a step as though I'd physically hit her. Did she think no one would have noticed her behavior at the dance? She was very much mistaken if she had! Spinning away, I continued to walk away, content to let her think on that.

All of a sudden, a hand was on my shoulder, and I was jerked around. "How dare you threaten me!" Anna said, fury contorting her face. "Who do you think you are?"

In hindsight, I could see how my words could have been taken as a threat, and I suppose a small part of me had intended them that way. Still, Anna was behaving like a spoiled child who wasn't getting her way.

"Let go of me!" I said, dropping my sketchbook to shove her away.

In return, she shoved me, and I reeled back several steps. Anna was stronger than I would have expected. She moved as though she were going to come at me again, but she was stopped by a small figure coming between us.

Tears were running down Katie's face as she hit Anna's legs. Shocked, my step-sister stared at Katie, trying to grab the small fists that were attacking her. Then, she twisted around, and I followed her gaze.

Father stood on the porch, his arms crossed. "Come here. Now."

Chapter Nineteen

When I was a child, I'd stood before my father more times than I could remember, guilty of some misdeed. Though it had been some time since I'd last been in such a position, the feeling was the same at sixteen as it had been when I was six.

Anna and I stood side by side in front of Father. He'd sent off Katie and Sam with Susan. My mind flashed back to the times I'd stood before him, and he'd made sure it was just him and me. It was a kindness of a sort not to scold us in front of the younger children.

"What seems to be the problem?" Father asked, his gaze shifting from me to Anna and then back. In his hand was the balled up paper Anna and I had used. He hadn't smoothed it out yet, though I expected he would at some time. What would he make of Anna's words? Surely, he must know her handwriting.

My mind racing to find the right way to explain without making it seem as though I were pointing fingers, I glanced over at Anna. From the way her hands were curled into fists at her sides, I knew she was furious still. She didn't say a word, no doubt trying to work out how to spin our confrontation in a way that put me in a bad light.

Father waved his hand to get my attention. "I'm waiting."

"All I did was ask if she wanted to have her beau to dinner," I said since Anna hadn't spoken up. I didn't even sign the words since it wouldn't have mattered. Though the last thing I wanted was to be the one telling tales, I wasn't going to let myself feel guilty for speaking the truth. "She didn't like it, and she pushed me when I started to walk away."

Father's eyebrow quirked up, and he shifted his gaze to my step-sister. "Anna? What beau?"

Even though it was rude and from the side it would be harder to read her lips, I glanced over to see what Anna would say. Her cheeks were flushed deep red, whether from embarrassment or anger was hard to tell. She began to speak, and her hands gestured sharply as if to emphasize her words.

It was difficult to gauge just what Father was thinking. His forehead was furrowed, and his arms remained crossed. He shook his head once. "Ivy, where did you see Anna's beau?"

"At the dance," I said simply. "She was outside with him after dark."

Again, Father focused on Anna. Beyond him, I saw the front door open, and Cordelia stepped out. Had we been too loud and disturbed her? She was in her nightgown with a dressing gown over it.

"What...going on?" she asked, her eyes flicking from person to person. Her expression was one of tired annoyance.

Immediately, Anna relaxed her hands and rushed forward. It was impossible to see what she was saying, but Cordelia's face revealed her feelings about what was being said. She was furious, but not, as it turned out, at her daughter.

She was furious with *me*.

"Control your daughter," Cordelia said, her gaze going to Father. "Didn't I warn you?"

Goodness, what had Anna said to turn this situation on me? I lifted my chin, waiting to see what Father's reaction would be. Would he side with his wife and Anna as he had in the past? Or would his sense of fairness, that I'd known as a child, return?

As Father glanced from me to his wife and then to Anna, I felt a small bit of pity for him. To be caught between the three of us was not a position to envy. He had a responsibility to each of us.

"Are you listening?" I saw Cordelia say. Wait, which one of them was she asking? She couldn't possibly mean me, could she? In spite of everything, a laugh threatened to bubble up in my throat at the idea.

Father pinched the bridge of his nose, and his shoulders heaved as though he were sighing. He faced me, and I braced myself for whatever was about to come. "Thank you, Ivy." As he spoke the words, he brought his hand up to his mouth and moved it out in a familiar gesture. "I've heard enough. You may go."

My breath caught in my throat, and I couldn't make my feet move. He'd just signed "thank you" just as I had a thousand times since coming West. Tears welled up in my eyes. Not only had Father noticed but he had remembered!

I wasn't the only one surprised. Cordelia's eyes widened, and she pressed her lips into a thin line. She didn't stay out of the conversation for long. "I should have known," I saw her say. "Vow or not, you...put her before your own wife...wishes."

Anna spun around and pointed at me. "She...never liked me! She's making up stories!"

Oh, so that was her story. I didn't even try to keep from rolling my eyes. As if I didn't I have enough to be concerned with than to make up ways to make her miserable.

"Who—" Though I lost the rest of Father's sentence when he turned, I was able to see my step-sister's face. Her expression was one of surprise and uncertainty. She shook her head, and her lips parted. Whatever she intended to say, a word didn't leave her lips, and her mouth closed abruptly.

"Anna is not a liar!" Cordelia said, putting her arm around her daughter's shoulders. She shifted her glare from my father to me. "Your daughter has...but cause trouble!"

Why wasn't I surprised that she saw me as the source of the family's problems? I gave a huff and crossed my arms. Father may have dismissed me, but I knew if I left, I wouldn't know how the conversation turned out. Of course, with Father facing away from me, I would only have part of the information.

Cordelia's arm dropped from Anna's shoulders, and she stepped forward. "So, you believe her over Anna?" she asked, her eyes on Father.

A warm feeling spread through my heart. Father believed me? Why? After everything that had happened and how he had ignored what I had been enduring, why did he believe me now?

Turning so that he faced me as well, Father spoke with slow care. "Ivy has never lied to me. Why would she start now?"

Once again, tears blurred my vision, and my hand stole to my pocket. Maybe, just maybe, I wouldn't need to take refuge with my brother.

Anna spun and started toward the ladder. She came to a halt and, after a long moment of hesitation, she faced Father once again. Her cheeks were an even deeper red than before, which made me think she was embarrassed and angry. For a moment, her gaze shifted from Father to her mother.

"It...nothing," she finally said. "Jack and I...talked. Ivy had no right to stick her nose in."

Father shook his head, rubbing his temples. At the same time, Cordelia took a step back, one hand on her belly and the other at her back. "Jack who?" she asked. "Anna?"

My step-sister shrugged as if she didn't know or care, and put her hands on her hips. "It was nothing. What...it matter?" She sent me an accusing glare.

Twisting around, Father glanced at me. "You may go, Ivy."

To ignore a second dismissal would have been rude. I gave a nod and hurried down the steps. It was enough to know that Father believed me, and he'd signed to me.

WITH NO FURTHER INTERRUPTIONS, I passed the afternoon in peace. The Montana mountains took shape under the tip of my charcoal pencil and spread across my paper.

To be honest, though, I spent more time staring off into space.

Cordelia and Anna did not join the rest of the family for dinner. I was able to put together a simple meal that seemed to satisfy everyone. If Remy noticed the air of tension, he didn't say anything in my sight or show any curiosity in his expression.

As if nothing had happened, Father opened up his accounts books once again. After I made sure Susan had put away the clean dishes, I sat down beside my father. When he glanced in my direction, I signed, "May I help you?"

He shook his head, confusion making his brow furrow. Patiently, I picked up his pen and used the paper he'd written figures on to explain myself.

Father, I like numbers. Mathematics was one of my best subjects in school. Please let me help.

The corners of Father's lips quirked up as he read my words. He sent a glance at the closed bedroom door and then shifted the book so that it was facing me. His smile had an indulgent edge to it, similar to one he would have when Katie tried to impress him with something.

For me, the hardest part was deciphering the cramped handwriting on each line. I could make out Father's easily enough, but the other two styles of handwriting took some thought.

I saw Father watching me work with an increasingly astonished expression.

Adding and subtracting the numbers was a breeze, and the picture they painted was both reassuring and concerning. It reassured me because the store had been doing well in the time since I last balanced the books in secret.

My concern, however, came from the fact that on multiple days in the past three weeks, the money the store brought in did not match the funds on hand when the store closed. Most days, the amount was no more than fifty cents, but it added up over time. Twice I saw instances where two dollars were missing.

Someone was taking money from the store.

I checked the numbers a second time to be sure. When I moved to do them a third time, Father stopped me, a frown on his face. I pointed to the first discrepancy, one which was for a nickel. He shrugged his shoulders.

"It happens," he said.

Moving my finger down the line, I showed him the second, and then the third instances. His expression became grave as my finger kept sliding across the paper. He grabbed the pen from me and began to scribble the numbers down himself.

Katie tugged on my arm to get my attention, and I turned in my seat to face her. She held the doll I'd given her in one hand and a wooden soldier in the other. A wide grin on her face, she made the toys dance together. I forced a smile and nodded, which was enough to make her run back to Susan.

When I twisted back around, Father's face held anger and disappointment. He was scrawling a message for me on the scrap paper. Once he finished, he pushed it to me.

I will handle this, Ivy. Do not mention what you saw to anyone.

Surprised by the command, I gave a nod. Of course, I understood why Father wouldn't want it known someone had been taking money. The only person I could have told would have been Remy, and he didn't seem like the kind of person who would tell tales. I would respect my father's decision.

Father closed the book and capped the ink. He made the sign for thank you once again as he stood up. Book in hand, he went to the bedroom door.

Breathing out, still in shock that Father had signed to me, I leaned back in the chair and considered the information. As far as I knew, Simon and Anna were the only ones who worked in Father's store. Had one of them taken the money?

Although my step-sister had been mean-spirited, what reason would she have to steal? If she didn't, though, it meant Simon was the person responsible. He wouldn't have, would he? Or had he been planning to leave for awhile, and this was how he intended to afford to do so?

Unsettled, I closed my eyes. As mean as it might have been, I hoped it was Anna.

ONCE AGAIN, CORDELIA did not come to the table for breakfast. Anna took charge of making the meal, glaring at me when I attempted to help. I left her to it and went with Susan to care for the morning chores.

To my surprise, Father took Anna with him when he left for town. With Simon doing...well, whatever my brother had been doing since he'd left, I supposed there was no choice.

Still, I couldn't help but feel a sliver of resentment that the family laundry was being left to me.

At least Anna wouldn't be there to overheat the water and "accidentally" splash me with it.

Susan was kind enough to gather up the clothes while I poured water into the pots on the stove. What would I have done if my younger step-sister had the same hatred that her older sister had?

I was just about to carry the hot water out when Katie came running towards me. Her brown eyes were wide with alarm. Her lips were moving, but I couldn't understand what she was trying to tell me. She pointed back at the bedroom door which was now ajar. Grasping my skirt, the young girl tugged as hard as she could.

Was Cordelia in trouble?

A glance revealed that Susan was not inside the house. Deciding it would take too much time to find her and convince her to check on her mother, I untangled Katie's fingers from the skirt of my dress and hurried with her to the bedroom door. Out of courtesy, I rapped my knuckles against the wood as I pushed it open.

My breath caught in my throat as I took in the scene before me. Cordelia was on her knees by the bed. She was still in her nightgown, and the quilt was bunched up in her grasp. Her shoulders were heaving like she was trying to catch her breath as she lifted her head.

"Idiot girl," she said, her face contorted with pain.

Had she called for help? Surely, even if she were outside, Susan would have heard her. Uncertain what I should do, I stayed in the doorway, holding Katie from running to her mother.

"Don't...stand there! Get—" Cordelia broke off her sentence, doubling over. I could guess what she intended to say, though, and why.

She needed help because the baby was coming.

Panic bubbled up as I pulled Katie away from the bedroom. What was one supposed to do when a pregnant woman went into labor? I had no idea whatsoever, but maybe Susan would remember how it was when Katie and Sam were born.

Grasping Katie's shoulders, I spun her to face the door. "Get Susan!"

Katie didn't need any more urging, and she ran to the door. Taking a deep breath, I sent a glance to where I'd last seen Sam, in a corner knocking over the wooden soldiers. Thankfully, he was still there, unconcerned with anything beyond the toys he had in front of him.

What was I going to do next? Even if Susan knew what to expect, she was not much past a child herself. We needed an adult, and the only way to get one was to leave the ranch.

Chapter Twenty

Susan ran in, panic written on her face. I stepped in front of her before she could continue to the bedroom. "Do you know what needs to be done?" I asked, watching her face.

She hesitated, her eyes shifting to the right as she thought. After a moment, she shook her head. "Anna sent me away before," she said, nodding towards Katie, who was holding her hand. "Do you?"

I shook my head, and her cheeks paled. There was no getting around it. One of us needed to go for help. Did the town have a doctor? I couldn't remember having met one, but that didn't mean one did not exist.

"Go to her," I said to Susan. If I'd lifted my hands to sign, she would have seen the tremble in them, and she didn't need to guess at my own fear. "Do whatever she says. I'll be back."

Susan's jaw dropped. "Where—?"

"For help." Before I lost my nerve, I spun on my heel and strode out. I didn't even pause for a bonnet or hat. There didn't seem to be a moment to lose.

At a run, I crossed the distance from the house to the barn in a matter of seconds. Why was today the day when there was no sign of Remy? I skidded to a halt in the barn.

The horses that pulled the wagon were in town, of course, at the store. Remy's usual mount was gone, and naturally, Simon's mare was no longer in the barn. That left only the massive black creature I'd seen Remy working with in the corral.

Somehow, I had to saddle and mount him.

Breathing out, I went to the small tack room at the back of the barn. I had no reason to be nervous. Simon and Remy had taught me how to saddle a horse...just not one that appeared half wild.

With a saddle in my hands, I approached the stall door. The horse lifted his head, and I made eye contact with him. When I put my hand on the latch, he shied to the back of the stall, which wasn't far at all.

Some instinct made me click my tongue. I couldn't hear it, but I had a vague memory of my mother doing so whenever she had dealt with a frightened animal. The horse didn't move, beyond twitching muscles, as I approached.

"I'm sorry." I knew I was speaking, even though it seemed silly. "I have to get Cordelia help, and I need you."

I felt clumsy as I heaved the heavy saddle up and onto the horse's back. How many times had I seen this creature lunge and buck when Simon had done so? For me, though, the horse remained still. While I knew all animals had a kind of intelligence, at that moment, I knew that horse understood the situation and was choosing to cooperate with me.

Maybe he was like the majority of humans and felt sorry for me.

He was less understanding when I put the bit of the bridle in his mouth, but he didn't try to shake me off. My hands were still shaking as I led him out of the barn. One last glance around showed there was still no Remy in sight to do the task instead, so I pulled myself up in the saddle.

My skirts were not designed for riding astride but were full enough that not too much of my leg was visible. Of course, it didn't seem like the time to be concerned about modesty.

I dug my heels in and raced out of the ranch yard. It wasn't difficult to follow the road toward town. How much time had passed since I'd discovered Cordelia? I couldn't even begin to guess, but I hoped I would be able to get help before it was too late.

The ground rushed beneath the black steed's hooves. All I seemed capable of doing was holding onto the reins. Eventually, I was able to sit up a little straighter, and I recognized the lane that led off to another ranch.

Pulling back on the reins, I managed to bring the horse to a stop. I didn't know for certain whether there was a doctor in town, but maybe...maybe another woman would know what to do.

Biting my lip, I guided the horse through the gate and nudged him into a gallop. It took only a few minutes to reach the house, and I once again brought the horse to a stop. A tall woman came out on the porch, drying her hands on a towel. She was vaguely familiar.

"Ivy Steele?" I saw her say, a frown creasing her forehead. "What's wrong? Come inside."

I stayed on the horse. Why did I feel out of breath? Beneath me, the horse's chest heaved. Remy was going to give me a talking to about riding the poor animal too hard. "Please," I said. The woman flinched. Oh, I was speaking too loud. "My step-mother...the baby is coming. I don't know what to do. She needs help."

A myriad of emotions crossed the woman's face: surprise, concern, disgust? "I see." Her eyes flicked around the yard as though she were looking for someone.

"I don't know what to do," I said again. If she wasn't going to help me, I wished she would say so right away so I could continue my search.

"Right." She gave a decisive nod as she folded the towel. "I may not...with her background or beliefs, but I won't...away one in need."

"You'll go to her?" I asked, sagging with relief.

"It is my duty...I never...." She took off her apron and then pointed in the direction I knew the town was. "You go on for your father."

My mount danced beneath me for a moment before he allowed himself to be turned around. He seemed more than happy when I urged him into a run.

Knowing that someone would soon be with Cordelia meant my mind was able to wander. What had my neighbor meant by Cordelia's "background and beliefs"? Since I'd never had a conversation with her, I had no idea. What was it that made everyone despise my father's wife?

SOON ENOUGH, THE EDGE of town came into view. I slowed the horse from a gallop to a more sedate walk. There were several wagons on the main street, along with people and at least a half-dozen dogs.

The hair on the back of my neck prickled as I rode toward the general store. I saw at least three men stare at me as I rode through the town. Was it so strange that a young woman would ride alone?

My mount—when all this was over, I needed to learn whether he was named or not —didn't like the change of pace, even though he was breathing heavily. He sidestepped and shook his head.

When I slid out of the saddle, I had to hold onto it to keep my balance. My legs were wobbly, and my knees were weak. Who knew such a long ride, the longest I'd ever had on horseback, would be so taxing? How did cowboys do it all day? Did they just become accustomed to it?

As I tied the horse's reins to the hitching post, a woman with a basket on her arm came out of the store. She nodded at me as she passed. That was the friendly behavior I'd grown to expect once I crossed the Mississippi River.

As soon as I stepped into the store, I saw Father and Anna at the counter. "Papa!" I said, half running to them.

In the middle of collecting some coins on the counter, Father paused and lifted his gaze. "Ivy?" he said, abandoning his task to come around the counter. "What are you doing here? What's happened?"

"The baby's coming. I hoped there was a doctor," I said, hoping I wasn't shouting at him. That wouldn't accomplish anything and only make panic. "I stopped at one of the neighboring ranchers and the woman there said she would go. I didn't know what else to do."

All color drained out of Father's face. His Adam's apple bobbed in his throat as he swallowed hard. He reached out to pat my arm. "Of course. Of course. Anna—" I lost the rest of the sentence because he twisted around toward the counter.

"Yes, sir," Anna said with a nod. As calm as can be, she hurried to the back. A moment later, she returned with my father's hat and jacket.

Without bothering to put either article of clothing on, Father rushed to the door. As he went out, he flipped the sign over so that the word closed faced the street. He vanished from sight, and I guessed he had gone for the wagon.

At least the situation wasn't resting only on my shoulders. I faced the counter, hoping that the calmness Anna had displayed earlier hadn't vanished. Comforting her would have been more than I could stand.

My step-sister's hands were over the register. She shifted coins into her left hand and then dropped them into the drawer. As she moved to go around the counter, I saw her slip her right hand into her pocket.

Had she just taken money? In front of me?

Anna swept past me, tying her bonnet on as she did so. Breathing out, I decided to wait for the right opportunity to tell Father and convince him to check the money in the register. With less than a day's business, it shouldn't be too hard to see if something was missing.

I followed Anna out of the store, and she made a point of closing and locking the door. She took one step out onto the boardwalk and came to a halt. Her eyes were focused on the black horse. After a moment, she spun around.

"You rode him? I have asked and asked! Will said no!"

It was still amusing just how many referred to the young cowboy as "Will" when he'd introduced himself to me as Remy.

"The horse was all that was there," I said honestly, and then watched the young woman's face contort into a scowl. Why was she angry with me? Although the right question would have been, was there anything that wouldn't make her mad at me?

Father brought the wagon to a halt in front of the general store. His eyes shifted to Anna. Whatever she'd said or asked, I had missed. Glancing between them, I saw my father shake his head. He set the wagon brake and climbed down.

He went to the horse and untied the reins. Once he led the animal to the back of the wagon and tied him to the back, Father then returned to the wagon seat. Relieved I wouldn't have to ride the horse back, I climbed into the back.

Her expression one of annoyance, Anna joined my father on the seat. Father slapped the reins, and the wagon jolted forward. At a pace that made the whole wagon bounce, we left the town.

AS SOON AS WE CAME to a halt, Anna scrambled down and charged into the house. Seconds later, the children came out, all three with upset and frightened expressions. Father vanished inside as well, not even taking the time to put the horses up after their hard work. Since leaving them standing in the sun didn't seem right, I decided it was up to me to take them to the barn, although I wasn't sure whether I should do the same for our neighbors' horses.

And how exactly did one go about unhitching a pair of horses from a wagon?

A wave of relief swept over me when movement caught my eye, and I recognized Remy. Shading my eyes, I glanced up at the sky. The sun was just about overhead. Had so much time really passed? It seemed that only an hour had passed since breakfast, but here Remy was for the midday meal.

When he swung out of the saddle, his eyes flicked towards the house, and he flinched. At least I wouldn't have to explain to him what was going on. Then, Remy brought his gaze to the black horse that had taken me to town, and his jaw dropped ever so slightly.

"Who...?" He paused and shook his head. "Did you....?"

"I needed to get to town," I said, my hands useless for a conversation.

"He is...ready for a rider!"

I could only assume he meant the horse was *not* ready for a rider. "He didn't give me any trouble," I said, wanting to reassure him. Well, not really. The most trouble had been when the animal had to follow the wagon. Father had been too concerned about getting to the ranch to notice how the horse fought to get free.

Remy didn't look at all reassured as he shook his head. He tied the reins of his mount to the corral fence and went to the back of the wagon. The black horse had had enough, for he reared up on his back legs as soon as he had the room to do so.

Somehow, Remy managed to get the horse under control and led him to the barn. Breathing out, I stroked the velvety noses of the horses still hitched to the wagon. I waited there until Remy returned.

I watched him unhitch the horses, appreciating that he took his time so I could see how to go about it. Although I didn't know what each part of the tack was called, I tried to commit to memory how it all went together. Who knew if there would ever be an emergency that meant I would need to know how to hitch up the wagon.

Once that task was done, I felt at a loss for what to do while Remy went to lead the neighbors' horses out of the sun. Should I carry on with the laundry? That would involve heating up the water again, which meant going inside. On the porch, Susan was building small buildings with wooden blocks with Sam. Katie was hugging her doll close to her chest, her little face tear-stained and miserable.

As soon as I sat down on the porch step, my half-sister was right by me, reaching her arms out. I lifted her on my lap, and she rested her head against my shoulder. Waiting seemed to be all we could do.

THE SUN WAS CASTING long shadows across the yard, but none of us wanted to go inside the house. Though I had no appetite, I couldn't imagine how hungry Sam, Katie, and especially Remy must be. I'd considered going inside and getting at least some bread, but every time I moved, Katie only clung to me tighter.

Of course, once the sun set completely, something would have to change. We couldn't stay the night outside on the porch.

All at once, Katie lifted her head, and she began to struggle. I let her go and twisted around. Father stood in the now open doorway, and as my half-sister ran to him, I scrambled up. It took several seconds for Father to reach down and pick her up.

Even in the darkening light, I could see the sorrow written on Father's face and a sick feeling twisted in my stomach. I held my breath, waiting for Father to speak. Remy moved over to stand next to me, which was a comfort.

"Your mother...rest but...will...fine. Mrs. Evers says she will put something together for supper."

At first, I was relieved that Cordelia was fine, and a little embarrassed that our neighbor was the one taking the responsibility of the meal. It took a moment for me to realize what he wasn't saying. "The baby?" I asked.

All Father did was shake his head.

Chapter Twenty-One

As hard as I tried, I couldn't shake the feeling of guilt that created knots in my stomach. Would the baby have lived if I'd been faster about getting help? If Susan had been inside and heard her mother call for help, would things have been different?

Though the stew Mrs. Evers set before us that night smelled delicious, I had no appetite. Father didn't join us but went to the barn. Katie and Sam, on the other hand, dug into the food with apparent glee. Susan made an attempt to eat, and Remy kept his head down as he ate.

When Anna came out of the bedroom, she was balling up cloths, which she dropped next to the back door. She sat in the empty chair next to Remy, and then...did nothing. Arms crossed, she stared at Mrs. Evers as though she were waiting for something.

Her lips a thin line of disapproval, Mrs. Evers set a bowl of stew in front of my step-sister. Without a word, Anna picked up her spoon and began to eat.

How could she be so rude to someone who had gone out of her way to help her mother?

Frustrated, I couldn't stay at the table a moment longer. Shoving my chair back, I stood up and faced our neighbor. "Thank you," I said and signed. At least one of us should show our appreciation, and attempt to keep good relations with our neighbor.

Mrs. Evers's face, which had been tight with disapproval, softened with a smile. She then moved to help Katie, who had knocked over her glass of milk. Anna certainly made no attempt to clean up the mess.

More and more, I didn't understand my step-sister. It was a wonder she had any friends at all if this was how she would behave around people.

Though I knew I should go to bed and get some rest, I felt too agitated to do so. When I wandered over to the back door, I could see the lantern light shining through the open barn door. It wasn't hard to guess what Father was doing out there.

He was building a coffin.

Leaning against the doorway, I closed my eyes. While I hadn't been looking forward to the birth of another sibling, my heart ached that he—she?—had died without a chance at life. What must Cordelia be thinking and feeling? Of course, life must go on for the rest of us, and it was useless to think about what might have been.

I'd done it when Aunt Ruth died, somehow, so I knew I could do so again.

A hand on my shoulder made me start. I glanced back, and through tear-filled eyes, I saw Remy frowning at me. Once he was sure he had my attention, he jerked his head up slightly. From that gesture, I surmised that he thought I needed rest.

Despite everything, he still cared. I managed a slight smile and brushed away the tears that had escaped my eyes. Briefly, Remy squeezed my fingers and then let his hand fall away. He slipped past me and walked out into the dark outside. I watched him enter the barn and then the barn door swung shut a moment later.

Father wouldn't have to care for his burdensome task alone.

There was a tug on my skirt, and I knew without looking that it was Katie. The girl had caught on rather quickly that she needed to be creative to get my attention. She blinked up at me, fatigue weighing heavy on her face, as she held up her arms.

With a sigh, I picked her up. I hadn't done laundry, so what did it matter if I woke up with wet sheets in the morning? If I took charge of Katie, then someone else would need to look after Sam, who was falling asleep on the floor. Anna refused to acknowledge me when I tried to signal her.

Susan, though, saw what I wanted. She slid out of her chair and picked up the toddler. Before she carried him to the ladder, she faced Mrs. Everson and said, "Thank you, ma'am."

Proud of the girl, I followed her to the ladder. Somehow, we managed to work together to get ourselves up to our attic with the children. We didn't get any help from Anna, who hadn't left the kitchen table.

Maybe she was in some kind of shock over what had happened, but I had the feeling that wasn't the case. In fact, I was beginning to be certain that Anna was a self-centered person who would never change.

IN THE MORNING, DARK circles were under Father's eyes when he sat down at the head of the table. He was still dressed in the suit he had worn the previous day, and the fabric was wrinkled. He sipped his coffee but made no move to eat the breakfast Mrs. Evers set on the table for us all.

Where had our neighbor slept last night? Surely, she couldn't have ridden to her home and then returned before dawn. However she managed it, she had a full breakfast ready when I came down, and the cloths that Anna had left by the back door were also gone.

Was it wrong of me to be relieved that I wouldn't have to wash the blood from them?

As young as they were, Katie and Sam seemed to sense the solemn atmosphere. The night before, they'd apparently been too hungry to take notice. Now, they both wanted Father's attention, and I was happy to see him make an effort to give it to them, though the bleakness in his eyes didn't fade.

Did he remember, as I did, the last time a child had died in our family? I hadn't seen baby James, my younger brother, when he died, but the feeling of loss was the same.

Though the food smelled delicious, once again, I couldn't eat. Had anyone thought to send word to Simon, wherever he was? Whatever the bad feelings between him and the rest of the family, surely he would want to know this had happened.

Only Anna behaved as she always did. She talked through the whole meal, though I didn't see a word since she made sure she did not face me at any point. Most of her comments seemed to be addressed to Remy, but he didn't give her more than brief responses. That didn't discourage her from continuing to talk.

Across from me, Mrs. Evers rolled her eyes on several occasions. At least I wasn't the only one disgusted with my step-sister's behavior.

All too soon, Father stood up. For a moment, he let his gaze travel around the table. Anna even closed her mouth, though her expression became sullen.

"Please...me at...trees...," Father said.

Please what? I shifted my gaze to Remy and, since he was standing up, I did the same. Reaching out to touch his sleeve, I drew his attention. "What?" I asked. It was clear I had missed something important. He was the only one I trusted to be honest with me and not be frustrated with my question.

Briefly, Remy's gaze flicked to where Father was herding the children outside. Anna followed them, flipping her braided hair over her shoulder. When he focused on me again, he said, "We're burying the baby out by the apple trees."

Though I had walked through it a few times, I hadn't paid much attention to the small orchard that was beyond the barn and corral. The trees were small and, as far I knew, hadn't produced any fruit yet. As far as a burial place, it was an excellent choice. The thought made tears well up in my eyes.

Remy laced his fingers with mine as we both walked to the door. Without letting go of my hand, he let me go through the doorway first. Side by side, we crossed the distance from the house to the orchard.

An oh-so-tiny coffin was already there, the lid nailed firmly shut. Father must have done so before any of us were awake to see. I could only feel glad not to have seen the poor baby's body.

But where was Cordelia? Did she not feel well enough to see her child laid to rest?

As we all gathered around the grave that had already been dug, I saw a horse and rider coming our way. When the newcomer drew nearer, I recognized Simon. So someone had let him know about the tragedy.

He dismounted and took his hat off as he joined us. Simon came to my side, and took my free hand, giving it a comforting squeeze. His eyes were somber and sad.

To my right, on the other side of Remy, Susan held Sam in her arms and had Katie clutching her leg. Mrs. Evers had her hand on Susan's shoulder. Anna stood a few yards away, her arms crossed and a bored expression on her face.

Did she have no heart? What had happened in her life to make her so careless and cruel?

Father glanced around at us all as he opened his Bible. He began to read a passage, and I caught just enough of the words, "shepherd," "want," "green pastures," to guess what he was reading. The book of Psalms, chapter twenty-three.

Once he finished reading the Psalm, Father then bowed his head to offer a prayer. Unable to see his lips to know what he said, I allowed my mind to wander. This had to be the first funeral I'd ever attended. I'd been too ill for my mother's and younger brother's, and too young before that. Uncle Richard had forbidden me from attending Aunt Ruth's. Was this how funerals were conducted?

Too soon, Father straightened up and stepped forward. With Simon's help, though no words were exchanged between them, they lowered the coffin into the hole. As Father began to shovel dirt back into the hole, Mrs. Evers guided the younger children away.

Anna had already left.

The tears that had been threatening to spill since I left the house finally did so. I slipped my hand out of Remy's and ran for the closest private area: the garden. At least there I could pretend to be working.

I pulled at the weeds with too much force, the fragile stems snapping without the roots coming out of the dirt. Every few seconds, I rubbed my face with my sleeve since my hands were covered in dirt.

Lifting my head, I expected to see Remy, but instead, I found Simon in front of me. Pushing on the brim of his hat so that it shifted back on his head, my brother knelt down.

"You all right?" he asked, concern in his eyes.

Shaking my head, I swiped my face with my sleeve again. "My fault," I managed to say. My throat felt choked up, and I swallowed hard.

A frown appeared on Simon's face. "What do...mean?"

I waved my hand behind me in the direction of the orchard. "I wasn't fast enough."

Though my eyes were blurry, I watched as understanding dawned on my brother's face, and then his eyebrows came together in an angry expression. "Did they tell you that?" he asked.

They? They who? Did he mean Anna or Cordelia? I shook my head again. "They will," I said, covering my face with my hands. Holding back the sobs was more than I could do. "Once they've recovered from the shock. You know they will. And they're right. I didn't get help in time."

Hands caught mine, and Simon pulled them away from my face. "Ivy. No one in their right mind would blame you." He spoke each word slowly so that I wouldn't misunderstand anything he said. "You did all you could. It wasn't the first baby of hers to die."

Startled, I stared at him. There had been others? Besides Katie and Sam? Why hadn't I ever seen...? Of course. They had lived in town until I arrived and so any babies who had died would have been buried near the church.

All the times I'd accompanied the family to town, no one had never gone to visit the graves. Is that why Anna showed no emotion? Because she'd gone through it so many times already?

"This wasn't your fault," Simon said again. "If anyone says so, tell me. All right?"

He seemed so confident, and in turn, I began to believe him. Leaning forward, Simon kissed my forehead and then stood up. "Where are you going?" I asked, rubbing my face. "You're not staying?"

Simon just shook his head and walked away. He went to his horse and then ride away from the ranch. My heart sank even more. He hadn't mended things with Father. Granted, it probably was a bad time to do so, but I'd hoped.

How much easier I would have felt with my brother near me when I had to face Anna all day.

ONCE I'D FINISHED PULLING the weeds from around the sweet pea plants, I washed the dirt from my hands and splashed water on my face to remove the tear stains. Katie and Sam sat under a tree with Susan reading to them. I didn't see Remy or Father in the immediate area.

I entered the kitchen through the back door. Anna was nowhere in sight. Where had everyone gone?

The bedroom opened, and Mrs. Evers came out, a tray in her hands. Her cheeks were flushed an angry red, and her brown eyes had a spark of fury in them. Her lips moved just enough for me to realize she was speaking, but I couldn't read a word.

She slammed the tray down on the table with such force I saw the teacup rattle in its saucer. Mrs. Evers remained still, her shoulders rising and falling as though she were taking slow, deep breaths.

Was Cordelia being intolerable with the only person to come to our aid?

Sympathy surged, and I moved to the stove. I poured out a cup of hot coffee and carried it to Mrs. Evers. Without a word, I held it out to her. It was a small thing in the way of consolation and appreciation, but perhaps she would accept it as such?

Mrs. Evers straightened up, her eyes moving from the cup to my face. Her lips twitched into a slight smile as she accepted my offering. She sank into one of the chairs and sipped the hot liquid. The fingers of her left-handed massaged her temple.

With no one else around, it seemed the perfect opportunity to learn what I could. As I shoved down the guilt at taking advantage of a bad situation, I hurried to my father's desk. With paper and pen in hand, I returned to the table. Mrs. Evers watched as I wrote out my message, and her eyebrows rose as I slid the paper over to her.

Thank you for helping us. I know some of my family are not showing the kind of appreciation you deserve.

The corners of her mouth twitched as though she wanted to smile. She sent a glance around and took the pen from me. I waited for her to write a response, which she then slid across to me. What would I have done if she didn't know how to read and write? That was a possibility I hadn't even thought of.

I'm happy I was able to help, Ivy. I respect your father. He has always been a kind man and was one of our most respected townsmen. I regret that such heartache has come his way.

Wait. What made her say that Father *was* once a respected townsman? Because he had moved the family to the ranch? But that wouldn't have made any sense, because he still had a business in town. Was there something else that made Father considered less than respectable?

Mrs. Evers shook her head, and she reached over to take the paper back. I could only assume she must have seen my confusion. This time, she took longer to write her message, and there were times when she visibly hesitated. My foot bounced as I tried to rein in my impatience.

Your step-mother has not made any friends in Nevada City since she arrived with her attitude toward the past. I know time has passed since the war, and most of us were far from the actual fighting, but feelings don't vanish so easily. And not when someone insists that just because the war was won by the North doesn't mean the South was wrong.

Did she mean Cordelia? Was Cordelia originally from the South? Is that why no one liked her? Because she maintained that the South's position in the war was right?

Sitting back, my breath leaving my chest in a rush, I shook my head. That couldn't possibly be the only reason. Mrs. Evers tilted her head with a frown. "You didn't know."

How would I have known? I'd been told nothing about my step-mother's past. I could only go by what I saw with my eyes, and there was nothing to give away that someone was from the South. Not unless they were a former slave.

And even if Cordelia had made known her opinion about the outcome of the war, was that really enough for the town to turn their backs on her? How had she managed to marry Father, who must still hold firm to his beliefs about the war?

Of course, I remembered Anna's words about how a woman had to take what she could get and how I'd wondered if Cordelia had manipulated Father into marriage.

When I lifted my gaze again, Mrs. Evers was biting her lip. She took back the paper and began to write again. What more did she have to tell me now? Again, she hesitated several times as though she wasn't sure of the right words.

You may as well know the whole truth. Cordelia Conway came here, supposedly destitute, and for a woman who refused to take in washing and sewing, she got along with no trouble. Her home was visited by many eligible men, and we all thought she would make a match with the banker, but of course, your father was doing exceptionally well.

The implication in those words took my breath away. I'd thought Cordelia had married my father because of his wealth, but beyond that, I never would have suspected her of having a soiled past.

Her expression sympathetic, Mrs. Evers patted my hand as she stood up. She moved to the stove, leaving me to my own thoughts. Of course, there was nothing that could be changed about the past.

How was I supposed to treat Cordelia knowing what I did? Oh, was anything ever going to be right?

Chapter Twenty-Two

Mrs. Evers showed me the stew she'd started for our dinner, and then she left. There was nothing left for her to do, I suppose, since Cordelia didn't want her in the house. At least I would know her name when we met in church on Sunday.

Father, his eyes red-rimmed, and returned with Anna in the wagon late that evening, and I realized they must have gone to the general store. It made sense. Life must go on, the store must be tended to, no matter the tragedy that occurred.

Once again, no one spoke over the meal. Anna took Katie and Sam into the second downstairs bedroom immediately after supper. I would have had them sleep upstairs with us again, but it was not a fight worth getting upset over.

With Anna out of the room for a moment, I made sure to write a note about what I had seen my stepsister do with the money at the general store. I didn't wait to see Father's reaction when I dropped it in front of him. What he chose to do with the information, whether he believed me or not, was up to him.

My somber mood followed me to bed that night. Cordelia's past had come as a shock to me, and I wasn't sure what to make of it. Was she truly being hard on me because she was outcast? I would have thought her own experiences in life would have made her more compassionate.

How wrong I was.

Restless, I tossed and turned in my bed. Something hard hit my head. Sitting up, I realized I must have made some kind of noise and someone—it wasn't hard to guess who was to blame—had thrown a boot at me. Sending a glare across the attic, I rubbed at the soreness in the side of my head and, in a moment of spite, I put Anna's boot between my bed and the wall.

See how she liked it in the morning when she only had one boot.

With a sigh, I returned to my ruminating. Being obedient hadn't done anything to appease my step-mother's temper. Standing up to her had only made my father's life miserable. Was there no middle ground?

My thoughts drifted to Remy. There had been such sorrow on his face when we buried the baby. How many family members or friends had he helped put in the ground? There was so much I wished I knew about him, but there hadn't been a chance for us to really get to know each other.

Time, as I knew all too well, continued on. Maybe there would be opportunities, by means of body language and writing, to have a conversation.

At that moment, I couldn't think of anything I wanted more.

THE NEXT MORNING, I woke to the smell of hot coffee. A glance across the attic revealed that Anna and Susan were both still in bed. Curious to know who was already up, I rose and dressed in haste.

Of course, there was the matter of Anna's boot. I didn't want to leave it where it was hidden. My step-sister would be furious, and I wouldn't put it past her to destroy my things when she went in search of her boot.

So, I made my bed, retrieved the boot from beside the wall, and carried it downstairs with me. I went straight to the front door and dropped the boot there. There was nothing to stop Anna from going through my things, but she wasn't going to find what she was looking for.

Satisfied, I started toward the kitchen and came to an abrupt halt. Standing over the stove, was Cordelia. She glanced my way, and I saw her pale face. There was no trace of red-rimmed eyes such as had been on Father's face. In fact, I saw none of the grief I had expected a bereaved mother to have.

Perhaps she was still in a kind of shock?

Without a word, my step-mother returned to stirring something in the pot on the stove. Her shoulders were tense, as though she were expecting some kind of physical blow or an accusation.

Biting my lip, I went past her and stepped outside, collecting the milk bucket on my way out. I crossed the distance to the barn.

Father and Remy were already there, feeding the animals. I sent a smile at them both as I walked to the cow's stall.

Since that first disastrous attempt to milk, I had learned how to manage the cranky cow in the mornings.

Soon enough, I had a pail full of milk and a contented milk cow chewing on the hay in front of her. As I carried the bucket to the house, I saw Susan tossing grain to the chickens, the basket to collect the eggs by her side. At least, there was one chore I wouldn't have to do.

When I entered the kitchen once again, Anna was seated at the table, a cup of coffee in her hand. Hold on. Why wasn't she helping to make breakfast? True, Cordelia could be possessive of her kitchen, but after what had happened, surely she would appreciate some help.

A hand waving caught my attention and, setting down the milk bucket, I faced my step-mother. There was a scowl on her face, and she pointed to where the dishes were. "Set the table. Do...have to tell you everything?"

My sympathy for her dimmed. Without a word, I pointed at Anna. As Susan and I had done the outside chores, it only made sense for Anna to contribute in the house.

Cordelia, though, seemed to have other ideas. "Anna helps provide for...family. You are a burden." Her gaze shifted past me and, though I would not have thought it possible, her face paled even more.

Curious, I twisted around to see what had startled her so. Father was in the doorway. His expression, which had held so much grief in the past two days, was a mixture of disappointment and resignation.

"You don't mean that," he said, his eyes on Cordelia. "Anna. Set the table."

I saw Anna scowl as she stood up. Surely, she hadn't behaved like this before I had arrived. I couldn't see Father allowing her to do so.

Although, my father had surprised me this past summer with what he permitted in his house.

Cordelia pursed her lips and turned back to the meal. As Anna began to set the table, I carried the milk to the far side of the room to be churned into butter later on.

Katie and Simon were not in sight, so I moved to the bedroom to get them. Before I had gone more than a few steps, Anna pushed past me, her shoulder slamming against mine. Unsurprised, I came to a halt. If she wanted to take care of the two toddlers, she was more than welcome. Did she want to make an appearance of being helpful?

The not-so-subtle scent of the barn let me know that Remy had come in. Cordelia carried bowls of food to the table and sat down in her usual place. On his way to his own chair, Father put his hand on his wife's shoulder. I flinched as I watched her shake him off.

Had Cordelia ever cared for Father?

Susan entered, her shoulders hunched as though she were trying to make herself as small as possible. She slipped into a chair and kept her eyes on the plate in front of her. I took the seat next to her and folded my hands in my lap. Much to my relief, Remy sat in the chair on my right.

It was several minutes before Anna came out with Katie and Sam. For a brief moment, she scowled at the seating arrangements, since she ended up in charge of the toddlers.

I didn't need to hear to know there was tension during the meal. Cordelia said nothing. Whenever she wasn't helping the toddlers, Anna took every opportunity to glare at me, which was really nothing new.

Remy's boot nudged my ankle. I glanced at him, saw that his gaze was on the head of the table, and focused my attention on Father. His plate was empty, but he hadn't risen to take his leave yet.

"...plan on hiring John..." I saw Father say. His expression was serious as he glanced around the table. I did the same, curious to see everyone's reaction to the sudden news.

"What?" Anna asked, her fork falling from her fingers.

"The store can...be doing that well," Cordelia said, speaking for the first time. A frown creased her forehead. "Simon will see sense and come back."

Father gave a nod. "That is my hope."

He hoped Simon would return to work in the store, but he was going to hire someone else there in the meantime? Like Cordelia, I was surprised. As the only general store in the small territory town, of course, it would be busy, but busy enough Father could afford another employee?

"We do...need someone else," Anna said. "You and I can handle things until Simon comes back. We should...replace him."

Was she agreeing with Father or with Cordelia? I had the feeling I'd missed a few words.

"When Simon returns, Anna will not be needed," Father said, not even glancing at his step-daughter.

My jaw dropped. Father was replacing Anna? Because he believed my suspicions about her stealing from the store?

"What?" Anna shoved away from the table and stood up. Sam stared at her in obvious surprise. "But...why?"

"I believe you....focus on other matters." Father folded his napkin and placed it on the table. "I have made my decision."

From the way Cordelia, Anna, and Susan stared at him, I had the feeling it had been some time since Father had made such a decision. "What other matters?" Anna asked, her hands clenched into fists.

"That is for your mother to decide." Father stood up. "We...get into town and open...store. I will speak to John this afternoon."

He walked over to Cordelia and tried to kiss her cheek. She turned her head away, her eyes narrowed with anger. Father straightened up. Without another word, he continued to the door, picked up his hat from the nail on the wall, and left.

Her face bright red, and a mixture of confusion and fury on her face, Anna set Sam on the floor and hurried after him. The rest of us were left to absorb my father's sudden announcement.

Katie slipped from her chair and ran to get her doll from a small chest next to the fireplace. Susan glanced around once, her expression apprehensive, and then stood up. She began collecting the dirty dishes.

Remy squeezed my hand once as he rose from his chair. He gave Cordelia a respectful nod and left to start on his day's work. I helped Susan wash the dishes and put the kitchen in order. No doubt, Cordelia would need rest

My train of thought came to a halt as Cordelia caught my wrist. Startled, I stared at her as her fingers tightened to the point of being painful.

"This is you...fault, you...doing," she said, her expression filled with outright hate. "You are turning your...father against us."

Stung by the accusation, I jerked away. With my hands full, there was only one way to reply to that: with my voice, whether it was too loud or not. "You pushing him away is enough to accomplish that." It was cruel, but it was the truth as I saw it.

Her eyes widened. "How dare you!"

"He loves you in spite of everything. In spite of what everyone says about you," I continued, determined to have my say. "But you don't appreciate that, or him, as a wife should. I might be deaf, but I'm not blind or stupid. You are the one forcing a divide in this family, and now you see the consequences."

She stared at me, confused and angry. Spinning around, I walked to the far side of the kitchen and put the dishes down beside the wash basin. Susan glanced over, her face troubled. Regret stabbed at my heart. She was a casualty in the war being waged, and she had no escape.

"I'm sorry," I mouthed.

Susan bumped her shoulder against my arm and began to wash the dishes.

Had what I said been enough to reach Cordelia? I glanced over my shoulder. My step-mother was no longer at the table or anywhere in sight.

Sighing, I reached for the towel to begin drying the dishes.

THE WEEK ENDED WITH little change. Anna continued to go into town to help mind the store. Without too much trouble, Susan and I managed to see to the toddlers and to finish the household chores.

On Sunday, Cordelia remained behind while the rest of us went into town. My heart was touched by how many people approached Father to offer their condolences. A part of me wished Cordelia had come if only to see the show of support from our neighbors.

Or would our neighbors have held their tongues if my step-mother had come along? I'd like to think that they would have been kind in light of what had just happened.

In any event, when Monday dawned, life seemed to have returned to how it was before the tragedy. There were reminders, though. A few times I caught Susan rubbing her sleeves across her face, her eyes rimmed with red. The lines hadn't left Father's face, and I had a feeling they would always be there.

On Thursday, when Father returned home, he had two letters for me. One was from my dear friend, Nina, and the other from Mrs. Weston. I didn't miss the way the rest of the family glanced at the letters with open curiosity. After supper, I sat down on the porch steps and used the fading sunlight to read the news my friends back east had to share with me.

Right away, though, I realized something was wrong. *You scratch out so many lines, Ivy, I could hardly read a word you wished me to know. Surely it would have been easier for you to just start over,* Nina wrote. *Is paper really so scarce in the west that you must take such care? If so, I am astonished you do not think ahead to what you wish to write before you put pen to paper. Is the scarcity of paper you write to me about really that bad?*

When had I ever scratched out a letter to Nina? I was careful and thought about what I wanted to tell her before I wrote. Perhaps I'd scratched out a word, but surely that wouldn't have made it unreadable. Unless…

Someone had done it after I had finished writing when I wouldn't be able to see what they had done. What had I written that would offend another person?

Staring at the paper, I tried to think back to the multiple letters I'd written to my friend. What had I told her? I'd explained about my family's new ranch, the siblings I had met, and everything I'd experienced since reaching the Montana territory. There were definitely certain ones in the family who would have been offended by my opinions.

Then, who would have had the opportunity to alter my letter? I'd only ever handed them to Father and had never left an unfinished missive lying where just anyone would pick it up. Father wouldn't have changed my letters, would he? That only left one person. What if Anna had taken the letters to wherever they took the letters to post?

Did she have the audacity to open my correspondence and then make sure she scratched out whatever she didn't like?

You write to me so little, Nina had written. I wrote to her every week, though I knew it to be an expense. True, the mail system could hardly be relied upon, but if so few of my letters had reached her, and they were altered, what was to keep me from thinking someone had deliberately kept my letters from being sent?

As sad as it was, from what I knew of my step-sister, it wasn't hard for me to believe her capable of such actions.

How was I going to stop her?

The answer, of course, was rather obvious. If I didn't want Anna to touch my letters, I would have to ride into town and deliver them to the post office myself.

Remy didn't question why I wanted to go into town, though there was a concerned frown on his face. He helped me saddle the brown horse he generally rode. I suppose he didn't want me to attempt another ride on the black, whom I had decided to call Challenger.

This time, my ride into town was at a much more leisurely pace. I was able to enjoy the scenery as I went. Although I'm sure there was no real difference, being on horseback seemed to give me a different perspective on the territory.

Summer would soon be coming to an end, and I'd learned a lot about the harsh Montana winters. I wondered how Father intended to run the store when there would be blizzards and snow to keep him from leaving the ranch.

In fact, what had made Father decide to move the family out to a ranch in the first place? Since I'd arrived, no one had actually said the reason. I'd seen from the accounts that the general store was doing well enough, so it wasn't a matter of money. Was it because the house in town had been too small for a growing family?

Maybe it was a conundrum that would be solved one day.

The edge of town came into sight, and I straightened my spine. Last time I'd entered the town, I had no doubt I had appeared on the edge of insanity on the back of a half-trained horse. This time, at least, I would look like the proper lady my mother would have expected me to become.

As before there was a busyness about the main street of the territory town. I fell into pace behind several wagons which were also entering. I saw the blacksmith working at his forge with horses waiting to be shoed. Ladies, with baskets on their arms, strolled along the boardwalk in front of the stores.

I swung out of the saddle in front of the general store and tied the reins to the hitching post. Through the glass windows, I could see Father at the counter with two women. If he'd glanced my way, I would have waved as I passed. However, he did not, and so I went on my way without a pause toward the stagecoach office, which also served as the post office.

The men I passed tipped their hats to me, and I nodded in return. I even recognized a few of them from church. There was a large group of men gathered in front of the building. I realized why when I caught sight of the stage, racing into town.

Somehow, the driver brought the horses to a stop in front of the building. I well remembered such sudden stops from when I'd made my journey west. How long did it take to develop that kind of skill in handling horses like that?

Could Remy handle horses with that kind of skill? It would not have surprised me if he could, given how at ease he was with the four-legged animals.

Knowing it would be next to impossible to get to the office with the crowd, I stood back and watched the coach passengers disembark. They were all men, dressed in a variety of clothes. Two were in suits, wrinkled and dusty from travel. A third had an appearance as though he'd come from the top of a mountain, with a thick, bushy beard on his face.

Impatient, I allowed my gaze to drift across the street. That's when I saw Anna. Her back was against the side of the barber shop, and her arms were around a man's neck. They were locked in an embarrassingly intimate embrace. The man was in attire similar to what Remy wore from day to day. Was that the man she'd been with at the dance?

From where I was, I couldn't get a clear enough look at him to even guess whether I'd met him before. What I could guess was whether Father knew Anna was with the man again. My gut told me no.

Shaking my head, I faced the stagecoach office once again. All of the passengers seemed to have disembarked and whoever was leaving lined up to step aboard. Baggage was being loaded onto the top of the coach, and fresh horses were being harnessed into place.

It was all happening in less than ten minutes. Such was the nature of the stage.

I saw a young man crossing the street, and recognized the man who had been kissing Anna. When he was a few yards away, his gaze met mine.

For a brief moment, the man's brown eyes widened as if he recognized me. Though names escaped me, I was in general good about remembering faces and his I couldn't place. I let my gaze drop down, trying to spot some recognizable feature that I could use to work out just who he was.

He was dressed like any other cowboy would be: sturdy trousers, dark blue shirt, leather engraved boots....his boots? I couldn't resist stepping forward for a closer look. The swirling pattern from the boot worn by the stagecoach robber. Surely, though, more than one man could have the same design?

When I brought my gaze back up from the boots, no more than a few seconds could have passed. The man's face was clear of all emotions, and I saw his right hand shift towards his side where his gun hung. He was on edge, and that only cemented the growing sense of unease in my stomach.

If he recognized me, and I couldn't remember his face at all, I had to assume this man was the criminal. The mask he'd worn the day he stopped my stage would have kept me from knowing his face. At least, perhaps the sheriff would want to question him. Where exactly, though, would I find the sheriff at this time of day?

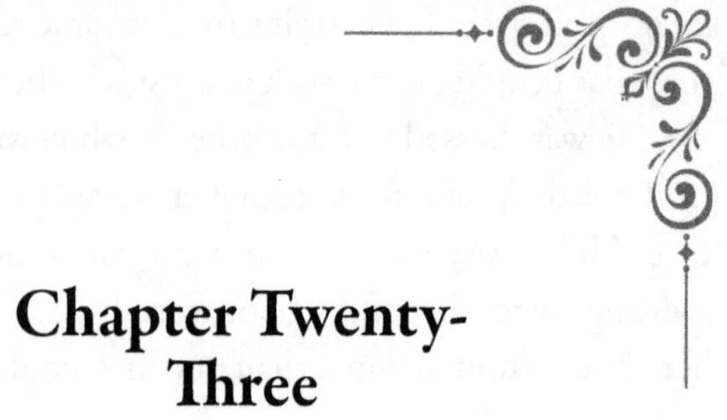

Chapter Twenty-Three

Forcing a smile onto my face as I would for any passing stranger, I started to turn. I flicked my gaze up and down the street. The sheriff's office and the jail were beyond the stagecoach office. Maybe Sheriff Worth was there, or even a deputy. In any event, I had to get there without raising the suspicions of the stranger.

As it happened, his suspicions were already raised. His hand moved to his pistol, and he was thumbing the loop away. Was he going to shoot me in front of everyone? In the middle of town? Did he imagine he could get away with such a thing?

All of those thoughts raced through my mind in a matter of seconds. Some instinct made me dodge toward the alley that was on my left. Something—a bullet?—sliced across my right cheek as I moved. All I knew was that I had to keep moving until I was out of sight.

After all, a moving target is more difficult to hit.

Not that it made any difference to a person who knew how to hit said moving target.

The wood wall on my left splintered, and I ducked my head once again. There were two large crates ahead of me, and I threw myself behind them, pressing against the wood.

My heart pounded in my chest, and both of my cheeks throbbed with pain. When I reached up, I discovered several splinters embedded in my left cheek and a long graze on my right.

I certainly hoped Remy didn't just like me for my looks.

From where I was, there was no way for me to tell if the man was still shooting unless I peeked around the boxes. I wasn't about to do so. Closing my eyes, I prayed some of the numerous men on the street had taken notice.

A hand on my shoulder made me jerk around and open my eyes. An unfamiliar man, his mouth hidden by his long beard, stood there. He held his hands up in the universal gesture that he meant me no harm. If he said anything, I wasn't able to tell for his beard covered his lips, making it impossible for me to read.

Concern was in his eyes though as he stared at my face.

"I'm all right," I managed to say. My knees felt weak, and my hands shook as I pushed myself up. "Is he gone?"

The poor man flinched. Was my voice too loud? With my nerves in such a state, I wouldn't have been surprised if I'd been screeching, though I didn't have the energy for that.

As I faced the mouth of the alley, I could see men running past, right towards the stage office. All of them had guns in their hand, and among them, I recognized my father.

"Father!"

At my call, Father came to a halt and returned to the front of the alley. The kind miner followed me as I rushed out. Father grabbed my arms when I reached him, his eyes wide with horror.

"Ivy, what are you...You're bleeding!" His gaze slipped past me. "What happened?"

His hands gesturing, the man explained. Or that's what I assumed he was doing. My attention was on the crowd that had gathered in the street. Of the man who'd shot at me, I didn't see any trace. Had he run? How had he gotten away?

A slight shake of my shoulders brought my attention back to my father. "What happened?" he asked, his eyes on me.

Before I could work out where to even begin, Father's gaze shifted away from me. I glanced over my shoulder and saw Sheriff Worth running toward us. The sheriff had his gun in his hand, no doubt in case anything happened.

He focused on me. "What happened?"

Paper. I needed paper. My hands were shaking too badly for me to expect any coherency in signing, and the sheriff wouldn't have understood me anyway. At the same time, I didn't trust myself to attempt voicing. Would my voice tremble and be incomprehensible? I wouldn't know.

I mimed writing, hoping it would be understood. Sheriff Worth gave a nod, though his expression twisted with impatience. He gestured for me to follow and set off at a quick pace.

Father squeezed my hand and walked by my side as I followed the sheriff. It was impossible not to see the crowd that had gathered in the street. Of the stagecoach thief who had shot at me, I didn't see any sign. There was no body on the ground, or anything to indicate whether he'd been apprehended or if he'd got away.

The thought that he'd escaped sent a chill through me.

In the jail, Sheriff Worth placed a sheet of paper on his rough-hewn desk. As I sat in the straight-backed chair, he uncapped the ink and set it in front of me. Breathing out, I flexed my fingers to shake away my nerves and began to write out my account of what had happened.

I was going to mail a letter, so I walked to the stagecoach office. There was such a crowd with the stage just arriving, I stayed back. As I was looking around, I saw Anna and...

For a moment, I paused. Once I put down on paper what I had seen, there would be no undoing it. I had to do it though and continued to write.

...a man who looked to be a cowboy. I was surprised to see them in an embrace, but since it wasn't the first time I'd seen my step-sister with a gentleman, I assumed it was her beau. When he started across the street, he acted as though he recognized me but his face was unfamiliar.

I wrote how I noticed the man's boots and the pattern on the leather. As I explained that I had seen the design before, had sketched them, but I couldn't remember whether I had shown that sketch to the sheriff or not. In any event, I knew exactly where it was in my collection of drawings at home.

The next thing I know, he was reaching for his gun, and I just ran. That's all I know.

There were more ink blotches on the paper than I would have typically left, but it was more or less legible. I laid down the pen, confident I had set down all the necessary details.

Sheriff Worth snatched up the paper and Father stepped over read over the sheriff's shoulder.

It was Father I kept my eyes on. His face paled as his eyes moved across the page. This would be the second time I was the one who had to tell him something negative about Anna.

While they were occupied with my explanation, the door of the jail swung open. Simon skidded to a halt two steps in. "Ivy," he said, his gaze landing on me.

There could be no doubt my appearance was a mess with blood on my face. Simon hurried to me, concern written on his face. "I heard...shots. Are you all right? What happened?"

"I am well," I signed and mouthed at the same time. It wasn't precisely accurate. My face stung with every move-ment and I felt weary all the way down to my bones. I ges-tured to the paper Father, and the sheriff was reading and trusted Simon would look to them for more answers if he wanted them.

He stepped over to the men, and from his body lan-guage, I guessed that he was asking for the details. I took the opportunity to close my eyes. No more than half an hour could have passed since I stepped into town, and yet, it seemed as though it had been an entire day.

How close I had come to losing my life!

And was I still in danger from that man? What was Anna thinking?

A hand on my shoulder made me start. When I opened my eyes, I found Simon in front of me. "Come...take you home."

Of course. Father would be needed at the store. He could not afford to be absent for long, not after having been closed not so long ago. Relief flooded through me as I realized I would not have to make the journey back to the ranch alone.

I pushed myself out of the chair. The sooner I returned home, the safer I hoped I would feel.

When, exactly, had the ranch become home in my mind?

Was it when Remy was so kind to me? Or when Simon began to warm up to me? I couldn't point to a specific moment but knew it to be true. The school wasn't home anymore; the Montana territory was.

Simon allowed me to go out first as we walked out of the sheriff's office. In the street, I saw at least fifteen men on horseback. I couldn't make out anything they were saying to each other. They seemed to be waiting for someone or something, and I couldn't work out what.

My brother's arm came around my shoulders and hurried me along the boardwalk. Whatever was going on, Simon didn't want me near it. We stopped for a brief moment in front of the store, just long enough for my brother to untie the reins of his mount and then we walked into the street, leading the horse with us.

We went to the blacksmith's shop. By a horse trough, Simon pulled a handkerchief from his pocket and pressed it into my hand. He left me there and hurried into the shop.

Leaning over the trough, I stared at my reflection. Blood oozed on my right cheek, and there were specks of blood on the opposite side. Dipping the handkerchief into the water, I dabbed at the blood, flinching at the splinters that were still in my flesh. I would have to find someone to pull them out.

Now that the adrenaline was long gone, I felt exhausted and frail. I leaned against the edge of the trough, using it as a support. My knees were weak, and I couldn't stop my hands from shaking.

Who would have thought after so long, in a territory as vast as Montana was, I would come face to face with the man who held my stage? How long had he been in the town? Had Anna seen him attack me?

So many questions and no hope of answers any time soon.

Simon came out from behind the blacksmith shop, leading his horse. My eyes shifted to his waist where a gun belt now hung. Where did he get that? Was the situation so bad it was necessary?

Without a word, Simon came to me and gestured for me to go to the horse I had ridden into town. He helped me to mount and then pulled himself into his saddle. At a trot, we left the town streets and headed east to the ranch.

MY BROTHER'S BODY REMAINED tense as he rode ahead of me. He constantly moved his head, keeping watch for anything out of the ordinary. Now and then, he would jerk around, letting me know he must have heard something. I never saw anything, though.

Of course, this meant that my return trip was directly opposite of my relaxed journey into town. I couldn't relax my shoulders and every time Simon reacted to a noise, I did as well even though I couldn't hear a thing.

As soon as we rode into the yard, I saw Remy working with the black horse in the corral. He twisted around and glanced in our direction. Whatever Simon called out caused him to climb over the fence and come toward us at a quick pace.

His eyebrows went up as he drew closer. "Ivy! You...hurt?"

"I'm fine," I said and signed as best I could with one hand. I saw Susan come down the porch steps and Cordelia out of the house. Good heavens, how loud had Simon shouted? I would have preferred a few moments to clean my face some more before facing my step-mother.

I was sure she would find some way to place all the blame of my disheveled appearance on myself.

Simon swung out of the saddle, and his hands gestured wildly as he began to speak. Remy, though, came to my side and raised his hands. He helped me to the ground, his dark eyes studying my face with a concerned frown. His fingers brushed against my cheek.

"I'm fine," I repeated as it seemed he wasn't convinced.

"That doesn't look fine," he said to me. He glanced towards my brother, apparently paying attention to Simon's explanation of what had happened in town.

Susan came running to my side, her eyes wide. In an almost kind gesture, she patted my arm as she peered up at my face. She grabbed my hand and pulled me towards the porch. Once she reached the steps, she let go of my hand and gestured for me to stay. Susan took the stairs two at a time and then vanished into the house.

Standing above me, Cordelia had her arms crossed in front of her. The expression on her face was one of disbelief. "..has to be...mistake," she said. She waved her hand in my direction. "She is mistaken."

Why was I not surprised? I could only guess that she believed I was mistaken about Anna.

Bowl and cloth in hand, Susan came out onto the porch. She stepped around her mother and came to me. Realizing her intention to tend to my face, I sat on the step to be more on her level. Susan set the bowl down, wet the cloth, and began to dab at my face.

Cordelia's skirts brushed against my back as she spun. From the corner of my eye, I saw her stride back into the house. Simon stared after her for a moment and then shook his head. He grabbed the reins and led the horses to the barn.

Much to my horror, Katie came running around the corner of the house. The last thing I wanted her to see was my face bloody. I must have made some sound for Remy spun around. He caught Katie and kept himself in between her and me so that she would not be able to see.

Somehow, he managed to herd the girl back around the side of the house. Susan spent quite some time tending to my face. I tried not to flinch when she used a pair of tweezers to pull the small, annoying splinters from my flesh. Simon joined us once he'd put away the horses, which surprised me.

Was he staying on the ranch until Father returned? Was there some danger he was meant to protect us from?

My thoughts went round and round in my head until Susan was finally done. Both of my cheeks felt as though they were on fire and every movement hurt. It was a relief, though, to not feel blood caked on.

As Susan moved to stand up, I grabbed her hand. I brought my hand up to my lips and moved it outwards. "Thank you," I mouthed at the same time.

She gave a nod, her expression unreadable. Without a word, she tossed the water into the yard and carried the bowl into the house with her.

My youngest sister was a mystery to me. She scarcely ever spoke to me but had never been as cruel as her sister or mother. What did she think of the situation? Did she long to be old enough and to escape the atmosphere of our family life, as Simon had done?

Katie climbing into my lap pulled me from my thoughts. Simon caught the girl's hand before she could poke at my cheek. "Ivy hurt," she said, her eyes round.

Looking a little shamefaced, Remy came hurrying toward us. How had Katie managed to evade him? He was usually observant and careful.

"She...like a fish," he said, spreading his hands out.

As Katie squirmed in my lap, I couldn't help but smile at the analogy, even if it did hurt. She puffed her cheeks and made a fish face. Beside me, Simon shook with laughter. A grin spread across Remy's lips.

For a moment, I was able to forget about what had happened and just enjoyed being where I was.

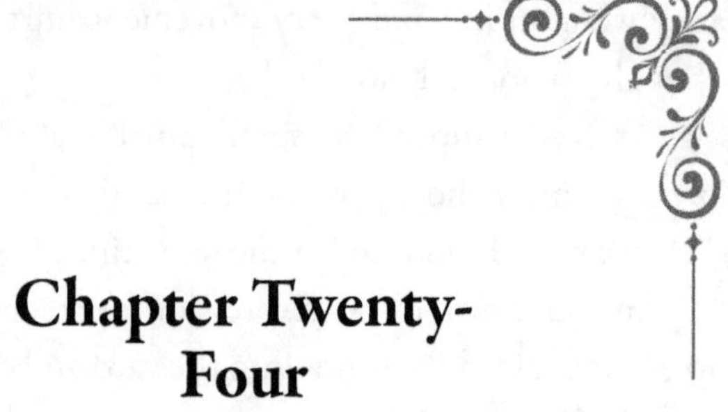

Chapter Twenty-Four

The day passed at a snail's pace. I couldn't focus on my sewing, the pieces of fabric resting in my lap more often than being worked in my hands. However, when I opened a book, the words failed to hold my attention.

Had the man been found and locked up? Was the posse still searching for him?

Simon remained on the porch with me, though I know there were several times Cordelia suggested he do something else. Remy returned to his work with the horse in the corral, but every time I glanced up, he was watching me.

It was clear the attack in town had unsettled the men in my life, perhaps more than it had frightened me.

As I shifted on the porch step, trying to get comfortable on the hardwood, I felt something in my pocket. Reaching down, I pulled out my letter to my friend, Nina. The whole point in my going to town had been to send it, and I hadn't done it!

Maybe it was just my nerves being high strung, but it struck me as the most hilarious thing I had ever done. At mere second later, though, it was a sober reminder and all urge to laugh vanished.

Slowly, the sun began to sink below the horizon. Though a part of me knew I ought to have gone inside to help prepare the evening meal, I didn't make a move. My book rested on my lap as I stared at the road.

When Susan came out to tell us supper was ready, Father still hadn't returned from town, and I had managed to work myself into a nervous state of worry. Where was Father? He hadn't run into trouble on the way home, had he? What if the robber was still out there?

Water dripping from his face and neck from where he'd washed and hadn't dried completely, Remy came from the barn. He held his hand out to me and helped me up from where I had been sitting on the porch step.

I didn't miss the way Simon rolled his eyes as he holstered the gun he had been cleaning and stood up. My brother went in ahead of us.

Remy rubbed the back of my hand with his thumb as he guided me to the front door. The meal was on the table, but there was no steam rising from any of the dishes. How long had Cordelia and Susan had the meal ready?

On the floor, Sam's little face was bright red, and tears were running down his face. I could only guess that he was the reason we had been gathered to eat without Father.

Taking Father's place at the head of the table, Simon offered a prayer before reaching for the first dish. His face gave nothing away as he passed it to Susan on his right. Everyone seemed subdued as they put food on their plates.

Cordelia, especially, kept glancing at the door as though she expected to see my father come through it at any moment. It was, to be honest, the first shred of concern I'd ever seen her have for Father. Did she have some affection for him, then?

Of us all, Remy, Simon, and the children were the only ones who ate without pause. I could only manage a few bites of the cold, glue-like mashed potatoes. My stomach was twisting inside me.

Because of where I was sitting, I saw the front door open first. Father, exhaustion hanging on him like a coat, entered. It was only when Anna, who was right behind him, pushed the door closed that Cordelia twisted around.

Pushing her chair back, Cordelia rose with surprising swiftness and rushed to Father. She grabbed his arm, and because her back was to me, I didn't know what she was saying. When I glanced at Susan, though, the girl was rolling her eyes in a way that made me guess my step-mother was sounding just as overdramatic.

Remy reached over and squeezed my hand, as though he wished to reassure me. What was being said that he felt it necessary to do so? Or was I overthinking the matter?

Father pulled himself away from Cordelia and came to the table. Simon pushed back his chair and rose, ready to allow our father to be at the head of the table as was his right. His face lined with exhaustion and concern, Father dropped into the chair.

Anna refused to look at anyone, even Remy. She didn't pause to eat anything. Up the ladder she went, and I suspected she would not come back down.

In a sudden burst of activity, Cordelia hurried to the table and collected the cold dishes of food. She carried them to the stove and began to dump the food into various pans, presumably to warm everything up. Ducking her head with a suddenly guilty expression, Susan slipped from her chair and hurried around the table. Her mother must have scolded her for not jumping to help right away. Poor girl.

Knowing I would only get in the way, I decided to remain where I was. I focused on Father and studied his expression. I'd thought him changed when I first arrived in Montana. Now, with the dark shadows under his eyes, he appeared to have aged ten more years in the span of a day.

Leaning forward, I disentangled my fingers from Remy's and patted the oak wood to get my father's attention. "What happened?" I signed and mouthed.

My father's shoulders rose and fell with a sigh. He shook his head. Did he mean to indicate that nothing had happened, or that he didn't want to explain whatever had happened?

Father didn't say anything else, though I kept my eyes on him so I wouldn't miss a single word. Simon sat down in a vacant seat, the younger two having abandoned the table for their toys in the other room. I saw my brother ask, "Did...posse return?"

Again, Father shook his head. Fear made my heart skip a beat. Did that mean the posse was still searching? Had they run into trouble? What if they'd been led into an ambush? That was something that happened, right?

Remy's hand closed around mine again. His thumb rubbed the back of my hand, distracting me from the questions in my mind. Though I knew I might miss something important, I dragged my gaze to him. He wasn't even looking at me, his eyes on Father. Did he realize what he was doing?

Cordelia came over, a plate of steaming food in her hand. I breathed in the delectable scent of fried ham and potatoes. For a brief moment, my appetite returned, but when I glanced at my plate, my stomach turned at the thought of eating more of the cold food.

Susan returned only to start clearing the table. Father didn't say anything as he ate his supper. Cordelia stood behind him, her hand resting on the back of his chair. I'd never seen her appear so anxious before. As Father continued to be silent, I wondered why the woman did not go to her daughter.

Of course, it was not the first time I'd seen a lack of affection from her. Did she know how to show love? Was she capable of the feeling? Or had she been so hurt by the world, by the war, that she refused to allow such vulnerability, even where her children were concerned?

Astounded by the idea, I stared at my step-mother. Was that the case? Why hadn't I thought of that before?

There was a gentle tug on my hand. Remy gave me a warning look. Right. Staring was rude, and Cordelia would only create a scene if she saw me.

Breathing out, I determined to be kinder to Cordelia no matter what she did to me. It would make life easier for Father, even if she did not accept the olive branch of peace.

Fatigue washed over me as I sat back. I didn't want to leave the table if there were a chance Father would say something, anything that would help me work out what had happened. There was also the fact that Anna was already in the attic. I had no doubt she knew I had told about her being in a man's arms.

I was not about to allow an opportunity where she could vent her fury on me.

So, I remained in my seat and watched my family. Simon drummed his fingers on the table, his eyes flicking toward the door. I could guess at his uncertainty. How safe would it be for him to ride to wherever it was he'd been living in the past few weeks?

Father stood abruptly. He took one step away from the table and then paused. "Please stay," was all he said. There was no mistaking the concern written on his face, the way his brow furrowed.

For a moment, I held my breath and prayed Simon was not clinging to his anger. Simon's shoulders rose and fell as though he sighed.

A few of the lines on Father's face eased ever so slightly. He nodded in return and then reached down to pick up Sam. Father carried his youngest child into the bedroom. Little Katie, her eyes drooping with sleep, toddled after them. I winced as she dragged the doll I'd given her. Each step seemed to bring the porcelain face closer to harm.

What could I have expected giving it to a girl of no more than four years of age?

Pale-faced, Cordelia entered her bedroom and closed the door. It was apparent she did not like to see Father anxious. Did that mean she had some feeling for her husband or was it all because it upset her routine?

Curse Anna for putting doubts in my head! It was exhausting to question everything and be suspicious about every little action.

Remy stood up, his fingers squeezing mine one last time before he let go of my hand, and left the house.

Simon focused on me, his expression grave. "..will keep...watch. Then, I will."

Anxiety that I hadn't realized I'd been feeling vanished. Nothing could happen with Simon and Remy to keep watch.

WHEN I WOKE UP THE next morning after a restless night, Anna and Susan were already gone. I took a deep breath and smelled the coffee brewing downstairs. As I sat up, I noticed the quilt that had given Simon some privacy was slightly askew. Forcing myself to my feet, I dressed quickly and tiptoed over.

I peered around the quilt and saw my brother sprawled on top of the bed. He was still dressed from the day before, and his boots were still on his feet.

The smile that came to my face made my cheeks sting with pain. I hadn't dared to look in the mirror before I went to bed, knowing I must look a mess. There was nothing I could do but let time do its healing.

Steeling myself to meet the day, I climbed down to the main level of the house. Cordelia was not in the kitchen. The back door was wide open, a clue that my step-sisters were out doing chores.

As I went out, I grabbed the milk pail. I'd become more comfortable with the task of milking, and had come to an understanding with the cow. I would never have imagined that being a part of my life, but there we were.

From the chicken coop, Susan gave a slight wave. The egg basket was at her feet, and she was tossing grain to the birds. The alarmed expression on the girl's face was the only warning I had before two hands were on my back.

I was shoved off balance, and though I tried, I couldn't recover. The milk pail tumbled from my hand as I collided with the ground. Without even looking, I knew who my attacker was, and I was amazed she would take a violent course remembering how my father had reacted the last time she'd tried to provoke a fight.

When I twisted around, Anna loomed over me, fury flashing in her eyes. If looks could kill, I would have been dead a hundred different ways.

"This...you...fault!" She stepped forward, her right foot going back.

Was she going to kick me? Of all she had done, that had to be the lowest of them all. I rolled to the left, desperate to get far enough away that I could get back on my feet. Before I could go more than a foot or two, Susan skidded to a stop in between her sister and me.

To my shock, Anna wasn't deterred and just shoved her sister aside. Susan hit the ground.

"Stop!" I exclaimed. No anger was worth hurting someone younger like that. "Anna, stop it!"

Anna seemed too angry to listen to reason. I grabbed her ankle and pulled as hard as I could. Arms flailing, she tried to kick at me but only ended up falling on her back. What a sight the three of us on the ground must have been. If I hadn't been so afraid of my step-sister, I might have laughed.

Still, Anna didn't stop now that she was down. She grabbed a handful of dirt and threw it in my face.

"Anna! Enough!" I sputtered, swiping at my face. It couldn't have taken more than a few seconds to clear my eyes. My insane step-sister had taken advantage and was coming at me again.

This time, she was stopped by a hand closing around her wrist. It wasn't Remy or Simon who had come to my rescue.

It was Father.

His face was filled with a multitude of emotions: disappointment, sadness, and anger. His thrust sent Anna onto her back. "Enough," I saw him say.

Remy came running. He went down on one knee beside me. "I'm sorry," was the first thing he said. His hands reached toward me, paused, and then touched my shoulder. "I'm sorry...in the barn."

He'd been in the barn and hadn't seen what was happening. It touched my heart that he would apologize for something that wasn't his fault. I let him help me up. "Susan," I signed and then gestured.

With a nod, Remy went to the younger girl and helped her up. Susan was clutching her right wrist, tears running down her cheeks. She rushed to me and put her left arm around my waist, hiding her face against me.

It always startled me when someone turned to me for comfort as I felt ill-equipped to give it. This time, though, she had been hurt trying to help me. I hugged her tightly.

My gaze shifted to Anna. She was sitting up now, her hands gesturing. I couldn't see what she was saying clearly. I caught a few words, though, "...meddlesome...harmless...her part....more right..."

Movement caught my eye beyond her and Father. Cordelia stood in the doorway, holding Sam in her arms. I was too far away to see her reaction to the scene. Looking half awake and rumpled in his slept-in clothes, Simon pushed past her. He came across the yard, his hands balled into fists. When Father held up his hand, though, my brother came to a stop.

What was being said?

Remy put his hand on my shoulder. In front of me, Anna's jaw dropped. She shook her head, her shoulders bouncing with laughter. When her gaze returned to Father, who stood with his back to me, all amusement vanished.

"You...serious? Because of her?"

Father pointed at the house. Slowly, Anna climbed to her feet. Her skirt was streaked with dirt, though I was sure mine was in worse condition. With her nose in the air, Anna faced the cabin. For the first time, she seemed to realize that her mother had been watching.

For a moment, Cordelia stared at her oldest child and then, with an air of finality and dismissal, she turned her back on Anna and went back inside.

Anna, it would seem, was on her own.

We'd been separated, but how long before Anna's temper snapped again? I knew without a doubt that I couldn't take much more from her, not without being tempted to retaliate. As much as I knew it would hurt Father, I would go with Simon, wherever he'd moved to, just to get away from my step-sister.

Susan let go of me and hurried to Father. She held out her wrist for him to examine. Remy stepped in front of me, blocking my view of the younger girl. "Are you all right?" he asked, a frown creasing his forehead.

"What did Father say?" I asked. Never mind how I was—nothing a little water and soap would not fix—I wanted to know what Father had said to Anna.

"Anna is leaving," Remy said, his eyebrow going up.

"What? Where?" Where would she go? Just into town to stay with one of her friends? Somewhere else? How long would she be gone?

"Far from here," was all Remy said.

I considered that for a moment. Far from the ranch would have to be good enough. My only hope was that she would stay wherever she ended up.

BREAKFAST WAS A TENSE affair, and no one spoke. Anna did not come down to eat. Immediately after the meal, Father went out and brought the wagon around to the front of the house. He remained on the wagon, waiting for Anna to come down with her belongings.

So, of course, that was when Sheriff Worth arrived.

The sheriff was covered with dirt from his travels. Though he rode straight and tall, there was a weariness about him that set me on edge.

What had happened on the search?

It was frustrating, at times, to have only questions, but often that was the case. I could only guess and wonder at things, especially when a good seventy-five percent of conversations occurred out of my sight.

Sheriff Worth dismounted as Father climbed down from the wagon seat. They shook hands and spoke together, though I was unable to make out a word of what they said. I remained on the porch, anxious to know what news had been brought and more than a little afraid at the same time.

After several minutes and just when I believed I would go mad with curiosity, they faced me. They both had grave expressions on their face, though Father appeared to be relieved as well. I clasped my hands together, wishing for the support of a specific person. But Remy had gone to tend to his work, and I needed to stand on my own two feet.

"Ivy," I saw Father say. "It's over."

The sheriff pulled a folded paper from his pocket and held it out to me. When I unfolded it, I recognized it as one of the many he'd shown me earlier in the summer. The face in the drawing was of the young man who had shot at me. What did the sheriff mean by handing the poster to me? I knew who the man was.

He reached over and tapped his finger against one word on the poster: dead. Understanding flooded through me. The criminal—Jake West, if the name on the sign was correct—was now dead.

A part of me wanted to know how it had come about, but it was enough to know I was safe from him.

Only...I sent a glance toward the house. Anna had been in the man's company. Did she have feelings for him? How would she react when she learned he was dead? Out of pity for her, would Father allow her to stay?

Breathing out, I handed the poster back to Sheriff Worth. "Thank you," I signed and mouthed so that he understood.

At that moment, Anna came out, a carpet bag in her hand. She was dressed in her Sunday best, the blue calico skirt sweeping the logs of the porch. As if to make it clear that she had not forgiven me, Anna slammed her shoulder against me as she went past.

Father's lips thinned into a straight line, his disapproval obvious. He took the bag from her and tossed it in back. Anna climbed onto the wagon without his help.

Sheriff Worth tipped his hat to me and rode out ahead of the wagon. I watched them leave the yard. Then, I spun around. The rest of the family needed to know the news.

THE SUN WAS BEGINNING to dip below the horizon when I left the house. I sat on the porch steps and watched everything start to dim. I saw Remy sit down beside me.

For several moments, we just sat with our shoulders touching. Then, to my surprise, Remy reached over and took my hand in his. His pointer finger began to tap against the back of my hand.

Puzzled, I glanced over at him. There was a pattern to the taps, but I couldn't work out what it meant. Sometimes his finger rested a little longer than other times.

What was he doing?

There was a smile on Remy's face. With his right hand, he brought up a piece of paper and held it out to me. He didn't release my right hand, so I reached over with my left to take it. In the fading light, I peered at the unfamiliar writing. Across the top was written: Morse Code. Beneath was each letter of the alphabet followed by a dash, a dot, or a combination of both.

I'd read about Morse Code before. Telegraph operators used it to send messages, and in the war, it had been used in different ways.

Still confused, I lifted my gaze. Remy's smile had widened into a full-fledged grin. In fact, I would have said he appeared to be satisfied with himself. His eyes, which were so much darker in the dim light, had a glint of excitement in them.

"So we...need light to talk," he said.

Need light? Of course we needed light so that I could read his lips or see his hands. Or...did he mean so we wouldn't need light to be able to communicate? The implication of the last made my cheeks burn with embarrassment.

At the same time, though, tears welled up in my eyes. For the first time, someone was trying to find ways to communicate with me.

Setting the paper on my lap, I used my left hand to sign, "Teach me,"

Even with the light against us, Remy pointed to the first letter: A. His finger tapped once and then again, for longer: a dot and a dash.

I couldn't resist the opportunity, and I waved my hand to get his attention. When I was sure he was watching, I held my hand up in a fist with my thumb free of my fingers. "A," I mouthed.

Comprehension dawned on Remy's face, and he nodded. He made the same shape with his hand and raised his eyebrows. I nodded, delighted he'd caught on. Though I had shown him several signs for things, I hadn't thought to teach him the alphabet.

Now we could teach each other at the same time.

I couldn't think of anything I would enjoy more.

Acknowledgements

This story would not be what it is without the help from a multitude of other people. I have to thank my mom for being my first editor, and my sister for providing the inspiration for Ivy. Thank you, Henrietta, for doing final edits, and Robyn for doing a final read-through to catch last minute mistakes. Thanks also to those in my writing group who put up with my periods of insanity. And giant shout out to all my readers on Wattpad who were with me along the way!

You guys rock!

Also by Bethany Swafford

Emily's Choice

Eighteen-year-old Emily Lawrence believes life to be simple and that the only challenge she faces is convincing her cousin and companion, Rosalind, to have more courage. This belief changes when Mr. Adrian Williams moves into the neighboring estate. Emily's father forbids her from having anything to do with the man, but when an unexpected illness throws her into Mr. Williams company, Emily finds that obeying her father is more difficult than she imagined.

Emily struggles to understand why her father is so insistent on the matter. What happened eight years ago, when the Williams left the estate? Is it a coincidence that Emily's mother died at the exact same time?

Coming Soon

A Chaotic Courtship

Twenty-year-old Diana Forester, a country bred young woman fears that her inexperience and uncertainties has driven Mr. John Richfield away. On arriving back home from London, she learns that he is already there, ready to continue their acquaintance. If Diana thought that it was difficult in London, courting takes on a whole new aspect when Diana's younger siblings become involved. She finds herself dealing with her own feelings, her sister, her younger brother, jealous members of a house party, a jilted suitor, and a highwayman as she falls in love with the charming Mr. Richfield.

Not My Idea (A Gentleman of Misfortune, Book One)

"LUCAS, YOU MUST RETURN home."

Twenty-two year old Lucas Bywood abandons his Grand Tour in response to those words from his father. Everything is not well at home and he finds himself in a bit of a fix. A little warning that his father had made tentative arrangements for his marriage would have been nice but Luke really wishes it had been anyone other than the young lady chosen. After all, Phoebe Ramsey had always been an annoyance and any time they had spent together had resulted in physical injuries for one of them.

Just when Luke thinks he's escaped that particular future, he finds himself courting a young woman he doesn't want, a furious best friend who wants a duel to satisfy honor, and the responsibility of finding who and why someone had caused an accident for his mother.

This was not his idea of what the summer was going to be like.

About the Author

For as long as she can remember, Bethany Swafford has loved reading books. That love of words extended to writing as she grew older and when it became more difficult to find a 'clean' book, she determined to write her own. Among her favorite authors are Jane Austen, Sir Arthur Conan Doyle, and Georgette Heyer.

When she doesn't have a pen to paper (or fingertips to a laptop keyboard), she can be found with a book in hand.To get notified about new releases and any news, sign up to Bethany's Newsletter here: https://bit.ly/2Hg7KJw

Read more at https://bethanyswaffordauthor.wordpress.com/.